HIDDEN ECHOES

Sakina patanwala

This is a work of fiction. Names, characters, businesses, places, events, and incidents are either the products of the author's imagination or used in a fictitious manner. Any resemblance to actual persons, living or dead, or actual events is purely coincidental.

HIDDEN ECHOES
Unmask the truth before it unravels you.
SAKINA PATANWALA

*To those who dares to question
the truth whispered in shadow,*

*For the one who wear mask but
dream of unmasking the world.*

In the influence of Gen Z era, where social media filters everything and everyone wears a mask of perfection or we can say tries to be perfect, we meet Eleanor "Ellie" Harper, a 19-year-old girl with a contagious laugh and has an ability to light up any room. In spite of of her outer charm, Elleanor has always felt out of place in a world obsessed with perfection. Beneath her bubbly exterior lies a curious mind, the mind which questions everything, every existence, the hidden truths of the world around her.

When Ellie moves to a small town to escape the burdens of city life, she came across a journal in the attic of her rented house. The entries, detail the writer's experience into paranoia, as they claim to be haunted—not by ghosts, but by secrets. The journal warns Ellie not to trust anyone, not even herself.

Initially coming to a conclusion that it might be a yapping of an unstable mind; Ellie soon finds her reality fluctuating. Strange occurrences started in her life:

A new friend vanishes without a trace.

Her image in the mirror begins behaving differently, as if trying to convey a hidden message.

As Ellie dives deeper into uncover the truth, she realizes that the mysteries are all linked up to a powerful tech company running secretive experiments on human perception. The line between reality and illusion blurs as Ellie discover that her very identity might be an artificial theory—a digital identity designed to test the limits of human emotion...

Prologue: A warning

The journal was worn out, its leather cover dull and cracked, as if it had spent a lifetime battling the elements. The pages were old and yellowed, giving off a musty smell that hinted at something scary. The handwriting was shabby, deeply pressed into the paper, as if the writer's hand shook with urgency.

The first entry jumped right in without any introduction or something:

"If you're reading this you're already at risk. Don't believe everything that feels real. Reality can be a weapon, a tricky illusion that ties you to a false truth. You might feel safe, but let me assure you, that safety is a trick."

These words dug a heavy weight in my heart, as if they carried the burden of unsaid stories. There was no introduction or any clarifications. Just a strange but frantic voice breaking through from the past.

The next lines were messy, ink smudged as if the writer had paused or interrupted:

"I didn't want to accept it either. At first, I thought I was imagining things- odd coincidences, quick shadows flashing out of sight, whispers that seemed to arise from nowhere. But then it began, the dreams. The gaps in my memory. The strange feeling of being watched, even I am completely alone."

The journal felt thriving, almost alive in my hands, raw with energy that made my heart race as if a wave crashed against the shores of my soul. The writer's voice rang in my ears, drawing me into reality that felt disturbingly familiar.

"They just want you to think it's just a paranoia they'll claim it's all in your

imagination. But its real they're out there, observing, waiting for you to be impulsive. And when you do, they'll change your life like a dream that you won't even notice what's missing."

In the corner a strange symbol took my eye off guard, a circle split by a rough line, resembling a crack in a coin. It appeared basic but intentional, holding a meaning that I couldn't catch yet.

The last paragraph sent chills down my spine. The letters grew bigger and more desperate, as if the writer had rushed to get it all out at once:

"Listen closely: secrets are key to unravel the web of lies. The truth may be dangerous, but ignorance will devour you. Trust no one—not even yourself."

The last word was underlined repeatedly, the ink so thick it leaked over the page. Just beneath, a shabby written page:

"If they discover this journal, they'll be aware of your search. And once they know, they'll come for you next."

My breath hitched as I flipped the page, my fingers shaking. But the next page was blank. So was the one after. Whatever the writer intended to share next would remain a mystery forever.

The journal slipped from my grasp and hit the floor with a soft thud. I stared at it as if it was some risky creature.

For a second, the room felt airless, and the shadows appeared to grow darker. The silence spread as if something really bad is going to happen soon, pressing against my ears, until I couldn't tell if it was my own heartbeat I was hearing—or something else completely.

Outside, the wind cried, shaking the windows. Somewhere far away, a lone bat screamed, its sound sharp and lonely in the night air.

A mystery to me, I had just stepped into a story that would forever change my life.

Chapter 1:
A New Beginning

The moment I entered Havenport, it felt like stepping into a postcard. The town chirped along the shore, with its not so busy streets twisted gently past charming cottages painted with pastel shutters and lively window boxes. The air was filled with the refreshing scent of the ocean, supported by a breeze that felt both fragile and welcoming. To me, this was exactly what I needed after the headache buzz of city life—the constant honk of the cars, the endless babble, and the non-stop radiation of the screen. Here, everything looks as if it is more peaceful and nicer, as if the time itself had taken a step back.

Even though I was here for short amount of time, I will make sure not get attach too much, but I can't promise.

Once the moving truck rolled away, I was standing outside of Bennett house which now was my new home. It was a little bigger than I thought—two stories, a tall roof, and a wide doorway that creaked under my feet. The white paint had seen better days at least, with a few chips and one painting hanging crooked, but it had its own charm. I can easily visualize myself near the window, sipping coffee and sketching the waves crashing against the rocky beach far off.

"Perfect," I whispered feeling overwhelmed,

Inside, the house felt clean but had gotten it worn of love. The wooden floors creaked softly, and a hint of lavender remained in the air, likely from a candle or cleaning product left behind. The furniture was basic—a baggy couch, an unsteady dining table, and a bed frame upstairs. It wasn't much, but it was enough. I have always believed in creating the best of my situations.

I opened the window and let the fresh breeze fill the room, smiling to myself. *This was home now.*

By mid-afternoon, most of my things were unpacked. My books filled the old wooden shelves, my crochet projects sat neatly in a basket by the couch, my paints were placed correctly by shades on the table, my other craft material were arranged below the table and my favourite painting—a bright forest scene under a golden sunrise—hung above the fireplace. In the process working I love hum softly, a habit my mother always said made her "impossible to be sad around."

With the sun setting, I had a thrill to explore. Havenport was small, like I could hardly see any human, while I was Wandering around my eyes caught a beautiful lighthouse and it was perfect time as the sun was melting in the sky, the scene was mesmerizing, I grabbed my phone and quickly took a snap of it.

As further I went, I came across the locals, they welcomed me with warm smiles as expected from small town people, though I noticed some had a hint of hesitation, as if they were trying to decode me.

"New here, aren't you?" an elderly woman asked, selling fruits at the local market. Her eyes were kind, but her gaze stayed on me for a moment that couldn't go unnoticed.

"Yes, I just moved into the old Bennett house," I replied cheerfully trying to be more approachable.

The woman's expression changed slightly. *"Oh,"* she said softly. *"That place has been empty for a while. Don't let the gossips get to you, dear."*

"Gossips?" I tilted my head, curious.

The woman waved her hand. *"Just old ghost stories. Small towns like ours love their tales. I'm sure you'll be just fine."*

I laughed lightly, brushing it off. *"Well, I'll keep an eye out for any ghosts then."*

But as I walked away, I couldn't shake the feeling that the woman's eyes were still on me.

That evening, I settled onto the couch with my laptop, already missing some part of the city, the city in which all my friends are in, the city in which I have classes to attend.

"You are here for a staycation, Eleanor, it's not as if you're going to live here forever" I said it reassuring.

my childhood bestie would love the town for sure, after coming to Havenport I understood why she loves small town so much, so I decided to text her back in the city to give her updates.

Hey, I made it! The town is so cute, like a movie set. The house is... unique, but it has charisma. You'd really like it here.

I paused for a sec, then added,

the locals are friendly but a bit strange. Apparently, my new home has a ghost.

Guess I'll need to watch for any spooky wonders. ;)

relaxed, I sent the message and leaned back in my chair, staring out at the skyline. The ocean sparkled in the melting sunlight, and for a moment, everything felt just right.

But as shadows grew darker and stars began to twinkle like sparkles, a strange chill settled over me. It wasn't just the wind—this was something different, something that made my skin cold. I shook it off, all thanks to the quiet countryside.

Still, when I went inside and locked the door, I couldn't ignore my sixth sense that said someone was watching me.

Later that night, as I lay in bed, my mind drifted back to what the woman had said at the market: *Don't let the stories get to you.*

"Maybe just trying to scare off a stranger," I muttered, turning over.

The old house creaked and groaned; its sounds loud in the silence. I closed my eyes, determined not to let my mind think of something stupid.

But just when I was about to sleep, a soft thud echoed from the attic, the sound which I couldn't ignore.

I legit froze on spot, my breath catching in my throat. Possibly just the wind, "yeah, just the wind" I said reassuring myself.

Yet, I couldn't help but took a glimpse up at the ceiling, my heart beats were a little unusual and with that I drifted to sleep.

Chapter 2:

The Journal

The other day I had that intense urge to have a look at the attic maybe the sound I heard last night was just a rat or the wind has shifted some box or any article up there but yet I couldn't shake the uneasiness.

I stood at the bottom of the narrow stairs that lead to the attic, flashlight in one hand and a broom in the other. The sound from the night before kept jerking my thoughts, like an annoying itch I couldn't scratch. I tried to convince myself it was nothing—maybe just a rat or some article I repeated myself—but now I was set to figure it out.

As I opened the attic door, it moaned in a way that felt almost cinematic dramatic, revealing a dim and dusty room that smelled of aged wood and lost memories. Spider webs were hung indicating no one has visited attic in a long time, and boxes were tossed around the corners like forgotten treasures.

"Great, this is just like a scene from a Scooby-Doo episode," I whispered.

I stepped inside, clearing away the webs that stuck to my face, it was disgusting. *"Why do attics always have to feel so creepy and spooky? Who thought it was a good idea to make the upstairs a haunted movie set?"*

The light from my flashlight moved around the room, landing on some loose planks set randomly in the corner. They looked oddly out of place, as if someone had just got rid of them. Curious, I kneeled down and pulled at the top plank.

"Please don't be something creepy," I said softly, jokingly, as I finally removed the last board away.

Inside was a deep hole, and there was a small object wrapped in what appeared like an old scarf.

Gently, I lifted it out and opened it, revealing a journal bound in leather. The cover was split and worn from years of use. A strange symbol—a rough line carving through a circle—decorated the leather.

"Oh damn," I said under my breathe, holding it in my hands. *"This is definitely something I shouldn't be touching."*

But of course, I opened it anyway.

The first page was mostly blank, but had one strange line written at the top:

"If you find this, you're already too close."

I blinked at it. *"Okay, that's pretty creepy and low-key I love some spookiness."*

I flipped the next page, where the writing began. The handwriting was wild and desperate, as if the person who wrote it was barely holding it together.

"They're stalking me. I'm sure of it. Every time I close my eyes, I sense them coming up. It's not just in my head if it's really

happening. The shadows move when I'm not paying attention. The mirrors—they're the worst. Don't trust them. Don't trust anything."

I let out a low whistle. *"Wow. Someone definitely needs to talk about this to someone."*

Moving to another entry, she noticed the words became more chaotic:

"Memories aren't safe. They steal them, twist them, fill up them with lies. Sometimes I wonder if I've ever believed a true believe in my life."

The page was scratched deep, almost tearing it in some places. my stomach did a somersault. There was something weird in those words, a desperation that made my chest feel tight. This person wasn't just afraid—they were utterly terrified.

"This is like next-level scary storytelling," I said aloud, trying to shake off the rising discomfort.

Sitting cross-legged on the attic floor with the journal on my lap, the more I read, the harder to stop. The entries look as if to be warnings to haunted things.

"The clock is wrong. I know it. Time skips, but nobody notices but me. I'm not crazy. I'M NOT CRAZY."

One page simply stated:

"They're in the walls."

A groaned left by my mouth, shutting the journal for a moment. *"Okay, whoever you are, I officially feel freaked out. Well done."*

But despite of my better judgment, well me being me, I opened it again.

As I moved deeper into the journal, the tone was now different. The entries became more thoughtful, almost philosophical:

"What is 'real'? Is it just what we believe, what we're told? What if everything we trust is a lie, and we're too scared to

question it because the truth would break us?"

I paused, tracing my finger along the edge of the page. The question swayed in the air much longer than I wanted to admit.

"Alright, Mr. Deep Thoughts, slow it down," I muttered, but my voice lacked its usual sarcasm.

As afternoon slid into evening, I found myself unable to put the journal down. Each page felt like a clue pulling me into a story, which I wasn't sure that I wanted to follow.

Then I came across the last entry, which struck my mind hard enough.

"If you're reading this, I'm gone. They've taken me, or possibly I've stopped existing. But I need you to know: it's all linked up. The shadows, the mirrors, the missing pieces in your memory—they aren't accidents. They're warnings. Don't ignore them like I did. Please."

Below that, in shaky, hard-to-read handwriting, were the words:

"It's not just paranoia if it's real."

I shut the journal, my heart racing. I scanned the attic, suddenly aware of every creak and moan from the old house.

"Okay," said it to myself, standing up and dusting off my skirt. *"This is getting way too strange. I'm literally done."*

But even as I brought the journal downstairs, assuring myself, I would forget it in some time, I knew deep down I wouldn't. the words were already creeping into my mind like a *Charli Puth's* beats that wouldn't leave.

As I placed it on the coffee table, my eyes were drawn to the symbol on

the cover again—the torn apart circle, rough and incomplete.

I had no clue what it meant. But one thing was clear: I wasn't going to let it go for sure.

Chapter 3:

Unwelcome Guests

I feel eyes on me

A presence I can see

Not just in my mind

The first time I heard the footsteps, I thought it was just the house being dramatic. Houses, especially old ones like them make noise. Creaking, groaning—it was all part of the small-town vibe. But when the sound came again, I was 99.9% sure someone's creeping around upstairs and the footsteps in the hallway are straight fire clues, I legit froze mid-swipe on my phone.

"Okay, not funny, universe," I whispered, adjusting my blanket tighter around my shoulders. I stressed my ears, waiting for the noise to return. But the house had gone silent, as if mocking me.

I let out a nervous laugh and shook my head. *"Get it together, Ellie. You're being a cliché."* Still, I couldn't help but double-check that the front door was locked before heading to bed.

The next morning, I was scrolling through my phone while sipping my coffee. my Instagram feed was a mix of pastel aesthetics, humours reels, and the occasional meme account I followed to stay "in touch" with reality. But as I refreshed my feed, the screen glitched—lines flickered across the display, followed by a strange symbol.

My breath hitched. It was the same jagged circle split in half that was on the cover of the journal.

"What the actual hell?" I muttered, tapping the screen like it owed me an explanation. The glitch vanished as quickly as it had appeared, replaced by my regular feed of influencer selfies and some creative painting.

I stared at the phone for a moment, my stomach twisting. Weird coincidence, I told myself. Still, I couldn't shake the feeling that it wasn't random stuff.

That afternoon, I decided to roam out to the local coffee shop. It was one of those cozy, indie spots aesthetic with mismatched furniture and a playlist that alternated between lo-fi beats and lit hidden track. I ordered a latte and found a corner table, pulling out my notebook to jot down some random thoughts.

I had barely took a sip when someone slid into the seat across mine.

"Elleanor Harper," the stranger said, smiling like they were old friends.

I blinked, my brain scrambling for context. The guy was around my age, dressed in a slightly oversized hoodie and jeans giving out vibes of some mystery drama's main lead. His dark hair was messy in a way that seemed intentional, and his eyes were sharp green colour, scanning me like I was a puzzle he couldn't wait to solve.

"Uh... do I know you?" I asked, raising an eyebrow.

The guy shrugged, leaning back in his chair. *"Not yet. But I know you. Moved into the Bennett house, right? The one everyone's too scared to touch?"*

I narrowed my eyes. *"Okay, first of all, creepy. Second, who even are you?"*

"You can call me Ash," he said casually. *"And before you freak out, I'm not a stalker or anything. Small town. People talk."*

I wasn't convinced. *"Right. Well, Ash, you've officially earned yourself a spot on my Do Not Engage list."*

Ash chuckled, completely unfazed. *"Fair enough. Just thought I'd give you a heads-up. Weird stuff happens in that house. Like, not paranormal activity weird, but... close enough."*

I crossed my arms. *"Okay, if this is some elaborate prank, just save us both time and tell me now."*

"No prank," Ash said, his tone suddenly serious. *"Just... be careful. Things in Havenport aren't always what they look like."*

Before I could press him for details, he stood up, sliding his chair back to place. *"See you around."*

He walked out, leaving me staring after him, my latte untouched.

Over the next few days, I couldn't shake the feeling that someone—or something—was messing with her. As the night crept in, the footstep returned, and they were straight-up bold. my phone continued to glitch, the strange symbol popping up in the most unexpected places.

Then there was the graffiti.

I first noticed it while walking to the grocery store. A faded version of the rough circle was spray-painted on the side of an abandoned building, behind the old peeling paint. It was almost identical to the one in the journal, down to the uneven line bisecting the circle.

"Okay, that's... unsettling," I muttered under my breath, snapping a photo with my phone.

Once I started noticing it, I couldn't stop. The symbol was everywhere: on lamp posts, under park benches, even carved into the bark of an old tree near the town.

Out of nowhere, Ash popped up like some creepy guy which is stalking me like a psycho obsessed stalker.

"Hiiee! Ellie, Wassup" he spoke with a contagious enthusiasm,

As he spoke, I stumbled a little,

"What happened Harper?".

"Nothing...I thought..." I paused,

"Anyway, what are you doing over here, at this time?"

"Fresh air: because adulting is hard and breathing helps" he said with a sigh, *"what about you?"*

"The small town's enchanting spell drew me in here," I said dramatically *"by the way you didn't complete our conovo from the last meeting",*

Ash was numbed but eventually replied *"you've just arrived I will answer everything when the times comes..."*

I was puzzled whether I should trust him and tell him all about the journal and the footsteps which I heard today but I just met him, I can't trust anyone this early.

Even if I shared everything, he might think of me as some weirdo.

"Ash, mind sharing your digits? So, I could reach out when I need your expertise about the so-called ghost house aka the Bennett house" I said sarcastically,

"Yeah, sure" Ash chuckled.

That evening, I spread the journal and the photos of the symbols across my coffee table, trying to figure out. The contacts felt too related to ignore, but the pieces refused to fit together. Solving mysteries is my thing. I can surely figure it out.

My thoughts were interrupted by a knock at the door.

I frowned, glancing at the clock. It was almost midnight. I debated ignoring it, but the knocking came again, louder and more demanding.

Grabbing a nearby umbrella—because it was the closest thing to a weapon I could find—I approached the door cautiously.

"Who is it?" I called out; my voice steady despite the knot in my stomach.

No answer.

my heart raced as I peered through the peephole. No one was there.

I exhaled shakily, locking the padlock and stepping away.

As I turned, I froze.

On my living room window, written in what looked like condensation, was a single word:

RUN.

my blood turned into ice. I grabbed my phone, my were hands trembling as I texted Ash.

"Okay, WTF. I need answers. Now."

The message sent, but there was no response.

I sank onto the couch, staring at the window, the word slowly fading away.

For the first time since moving to Havenport, I wasn't just uneasy—I was terrified.

Chapter 4:

The Disappearing Act

I was sipping my second latte of the day my obsession with latte was getting worse, when a random girl popped up, why is this town so random

"Is that almond milk or regular?"

Startled, I looked up. The girl in front of me wore a big solid hoodie, ripped jeans which seemed thrifted, and combat boots that had seen better days. Her purple hair was messily piled into two buns, and round glasses framed her sharp, curious eyes.

"Uh... almond," I replied, still a bit confused.

"Smart choice. Regular milk is, like, poison over time," the girl said bluntly, plopping down in front of me without a greeting. *"You're the Bennett House girl, right?"*

I blinked. *"Wow, is there a sign on my back? Why do people keep saying that?"*

The girl leaned forward, grinning. *"Havenport's a small town. We know things. Plus, everyone loves a good story, and you're living in our version of a spooky house."*

I raised an eyebrow. *"And you are?"*

"Mia," she said, extending her hand. *"Barista at Moonstone Café, part-time conspiracy theorist, and full-time trouble-maker."*

I hesitated but shook Mia's hand. *"Elleanor. coffee lover, expert in questionable decisions."*

"I like you," Mia said, her grin growing wider. *"So, tell me Elleanor—has it begun yet?"*

"You can call me Ellie and Has what begun?"

Mia's eyes sparkled with mischief. *"The strange stuff. You know, the footsteps, the cold spots, random shadow figures hanging around."*

I froze for a moment, then forced a laugh. *"Okay, that's not funny. Did Ash send you? Are you two pulling some sort of prank?"*

Mia tilted her head. *"Ash? Oh, you've met the town legend."*

"Legend?"

Mia nodded seriously. *"He's like a raccoon in a hoodie. Shows up when you least expect him, shares some legendary tale, and then he's gone. Classic Ash."*

I couldn't help but laugh at that description, though Mia's sudden appearance still made me not trusting her completely. *"So, if you're not messing with me, why are you so curious about my house?"*

Mia leaned back in her chair, crossing her arms. *"Because that place is strange. People talk about it like it's cursed. So many people have come and gone, but none seem to stick around for long."*

"Why's that?"

Mia shrugged. *"Depends who you ask. Some say it's haunted; others think it's tied to some secret government thing. Personally, I think it has something to do with the disappearances."*

I frowned. *"Disappearances?"*

Mia lowered her voice, glancing around like someone was eavesdropping. "*Yeah. People go missing here. It's not super common, but it's enough to raise eyebrows. The police say it's just accidents or people leaving, but I don't believe that. Something feels off."*

My body shivered; Mia's words felt too real.

Over the next few days, me and Mia fell into a comfortable routine. We met at the café or explore around town, swapping stories and theories about the odd happenings in Havenport. Mia had a way of turning even the darkest subjects into exciting adventures, her energy contagious. On the other hand, me and Ash were now on talking basis, we texted each other not frequently but once in a while.

"Alright, hear me out," Mia said one afternoon as we sat on a park bench. "*What if the disappearances are due to time loops? Like, people getting sucked into an alternate reality and just... poof."*

A chuckled left my mouth. *"That sounds crazy."*

Mia raised an eyebrow. *"Says the girl living in a house that seems straight out of a horror movie."*

"Touché," I agreed, unable to deny how much I enjoyed Mia's company.

Then, just like that, Mia was gone.

It started with a text that didn't get a reply.

I had sent a message asking if Mia wanted to hang out, but hours passed with no answer. By the next day, calling Mia but went straight to voicemail.

"Maybe she's just ghosting me," I muttered, pacing my living room. But something felt off. Mia wouldn't just disappear—she'd have left a yapping voicemail or come up with some wild excuse about aliens or something.

I decided to head to the café. When I walked in, Lucas, the usual barista, looked up and smiled.

"Hey, Ellie. The usual?"

"Actually, I'm looking for Mia. Have you seen her?"

Lucas's smile faded. *"Mia hasn't been here for a couple of days. She didn't tell you?"*

A frown came across my eyebrows. *"Tell me what?"*

Lucas hesitated, looking uneasy. *"I don't know; she just... stopped coming. I thought she was just taking a break or something."*

That didn't sound like something Mia would do.

By the third day, I was lowkey worried. I tried calling Mia again, but the line was still silent.

"Alright," she thought, grabbing the journal from the coffee table. *"Let's see if this has any clues."* Because last time when I was reading the journal one entry did mention something about vanishing.

As I flipped through the pages, my eyes scanned for anything related to Mia's disappearance. It wasn't until I got to the middle of the journal that something caught my eye.

"They're watching. They know when you start asking questions. The more you dig, the closer they get."

My stomach dropped. Mia had definitely been asking too many questions.

Then I noticed it. In the corner of a page, there was a faint, rough circle symbol. Underneath written three words, which said:

"They take people."

I slammed the journal shut, my heart racing.

That night, I couldn't fall asleep. Every creak in the house, every gust of wind outside made me jump. All I could think about was Mia, the symbol, and the creepy warnings scribbled in the journal.

At some point, I must have dozed off, because I woke to a soft tapping on my window.

My heart raced as I sat up, the room dark and quiet. The tapping came again, gentle but insistent.

I crept over to the window, my breath fogging up the glass as I peeked outside.

Nothing.

But as I turned back toward my bed, I froze on the spot.

On my mirror, written in what looked like ash, were two words:

"HELP ME."

My blood turned ice. The handwriting was very familiar.

It was Mia's.

The coffee shop was quieter than usual that evening. I was sitting by the window, staring at the journal I had brought along, but my thoughts kept drifting. The strange events, the whispers of disappearances, and now Mia's unsettling rumours were starting to weigh on me.

Ash slid into the seat across from mine, uninvited as always, but I didn't mind. He carried two steaming mugs, placing one in front of me.

"Thought you could use a coffee," he said, his tone casual but his eyes warm.

I raised an eyebrow. *"I didn't order this."*

Ash shrugged. *"Yeah, but you're predictable. Always a coffee when you're stressed."*

I blinked, surprised he'd noticed. *"Okay, stalker?"*

Ash smirked, leaning back in his chair. *"I just pay attention, Harper. You should try it sometime."*

The corners of my mouth twitched upward despite myself. I took a sip of the coffee and let the warmth calm my nerves. *"Thanks, I guess."*

"So," Ash began, nodding toward the journal, *"what's got you all moody today?"*

I hesitated a bit. I'd been avoiding sharing too much about the journal with anyone, but Ash had this way of getting under my defences.

"It's just... weird," I admitted, tapping my fingers on the table. *"I found this thing in my attic, and it's full of these paranoid ramblings. Stuff about shadows, memories not being real, blah blah. The kind of thing that makes you think the writer was either a genius or completely unhinged."*

Ash leaned forward, fascinated. *"Unhinged how?"*

I opened the journal, flipping to one of the more desperate entries. I pushed it across the table. *"See it yourself."*

Ash scanned the page, his expression unstable from curious to serious. ***"'They're watching. They know when I sleep, when I breathe. Even when I forget, they remember.'"*** He looked up at me, his voice lower. *"Okay, yeah. That's some next-level creepy stuff."*

"Right?" I said, my voice rising slightly. *"And now Mia's gone, and I'm starting to think this town is like, the setting of some messed-up horror show."*

Ash studied me for a moment, his playful behaviour softening. *"You really think something's going on like something weird?"*

I sighed, tucking a strand of hair behind my ear. *"I don't know. Maybe I'm just letting this get to me. But Mia disappearing like that... it feels off. And this journal, it's like it's daring me to link-up the dots."*

Ash tapped the table, his brow furrowing. *"If there's even a tiny little chance you're right, you shouldn't be dealing with this alone."*

I blinked at him. *"What, you want to be my sidekick now?"*

He grinned. *"I was thinking more like partner-in-crime. You'd be lost without me."*

I rolled my eyes but couldn't hide my smile. *"Fine. But if you start acting like one of those conspiracy theorists, I'm out."*

For the first time that day, I felt a bit lighter. There was something comforting about

Ash's presence, the way he didn't dismiss my fears or treat me like I was crazy.

we spent the next hour going over the journal together, active ideas off each other. At some point, Ash made a joke about how they were like Sherlock and Watson, and I snorted so loudly the barista gave me a weird look.

As we packed up to leave, Ash pushed my shoulder. *"Hey, Harper."*

"What?" I asked, slinging my bag over my shoulder.

"Don't stress too much. Whatever's going on, we'll figure it out."

His words stayed as they stepped out into the cool night air, the weight of the journal feeling just a little less heavy in my bag.

For the first time in weeks, I didn't feel so alone.

Chapter 5:

The Mirror's Edge

It all started on a Tuesday morning, just like any other day. Standing Infront of my small bathroom mirror, brushing my teeth. Half-asleep, my mind filled with conspiracy of stars, when something caught my attention.

The reflection in the mirror… it seemed delayed.

It wasn't by much—just a second or so—but enough for me to notice. I froze on the spot, toothbrush still in mouth, and stared hard at the mirror. my reflection stared back, moving exactly as it should.

"Ugh! You're losing it Ellie," I said under my breath, spitting into the sink. shooed off the weird feeling, finished rinsing my mouth, and left the bathroom, trying very hard not to think about it, but yet texted Ash,

"Dude, it's happening again!"

"Woah! Tell me the whole thing?" he texted back in few minutes.

"Firstly, cool down, it's just the mirrors are acting strange or maybe it's just in my mind"

"I'll be at you place in 5" Ash replied

My reflection in the mirror wasn't behaving normally. I swore I saw it smirk earlier, while my face wasn't. It felt like paranoia scraping me, but this wasn't the first time something felt... off.

It was late evening, and the house felt emptier than usual. Ash had gone out to gather supplies earlier, leaving me to flap in my thoughts. When he returned, I was sitting on the couch, staring at my hands, my expression distant.

Ash sat beside me, tossing a pack of chips on the table between us. *"You look like you've seen a ghost,"* he joked lightly.

I glanced at him, my frown deepening. *"Ash, do you ever feel like you're losing your mind?"*

His playful grin faded, exchanged by concern. *"What happened?"*

I hesitated but continued, unsure if I wanted to sound absurd. *"It's just... weird stuff. Like, I look in the mirror, and it doesn't feel like me. It's like someone's watching me, but not in a normal way. I don't know. Maybe I'm just overthinking."*

Ash studied me for a minute, then leaned back on the couch, his tone casual but reassuring. *"Ells, this whole situation is insane. You're not losing your mind. You're just reacting to a messed-up reality. That's normal."*

I raised an eyebrow. *"Did you just call me 'Ells'? Who gave you permission to give me nicknames?"*

He smirked. *"You're avoiding my nickname. That's how I know you're not losing it."*

I rolled my eyes, but a small smile pulled my lips. Ash always had a way of breaking through my walls without being pushy.

We sat in comfortable silence for a while, the only sound coming from the faint whisper of trees outside. Then Ash leaned forward, resting his elbows on his knees.

"You know," he said, his voice softer now, *"if you ever feel like everything's too much, you can talk to me. I mean, I know I'm not the best at... feelings or whatever, but I'm here."*

I looked at him, surprised by his sincerity. *"Thanks, Ash. That actually means a lot."*

Ash shrugged, trying to play it cool. *"Don't mention it. But, uh, if you do lose your mind, I'm not taking care of you. I barely know how to take care of myself."*

I laughed, the tension in my chest easing slightly. *"Good to know. I'll take a note of that."*

He grinned, then grabbed the pack of chips and tore it open. *"Okay, enough with the existential anxiety. Let's eat chips and argue about the worst series ever made or any worst book."*

"Easy," I said, grabbing a handful of chips. *"Anything with mafias in it."*

Ash gasped, mock-offended. *"Whoa. That's a personal attack. Are you talking about Dark romances? That books are masterpiece."*

I burst out laughing. *"Masterpiece? Ash, dark romances are so bad, I mean who romanticizes toxicity?"*

For the next hour, we argued, teased, and laughed until I felt the weight of my fears boost, if only somewhat. It wasn't a solution of my problems, but it recapped me that I wasn't alone in this fight.

As the night wore on, and Ash slept on the couch beside me, I glanced at the mirror across the room. This time, my reflection stared back like it always had—just me. No smirks, no unease.

For the first time in days, I felt like I could breathe.

A few days later, the strangeness came back, stronger this time.

I had spent most of the afternoon binge-watching a crime documentary, curled up under a blanket. Around sunset, I got up to grab my go to snack. As I passed the hall mirror, something made me glance over.

My reflection wasn't moving.

I froze mid-step. My heart started racing as I stared at the mirror. my reflection just stood there, arms at my sides, watching me with an expression that almost looked… sad.

"What the—" I whispered, but before I could finish, the reflection moved again, perfectly matching my position.

I swallowed hard, trying to calm my breathing. Slowly, I stepped closer to the mirror, waving a hand in front of my face. This time, the reflection followed perfectly, just like normal.

"Okay, you're completely alright," I said out loud, trying to convince myself. *"Totally alright. Nothing weird is happening, right!?"*

But the feeling stayed with me Something wasn't right.

By the time it happened for the third time, I couldn't ignore it anymore.

I was at my vanity table, redoing my eyeliner for the Nth time because the wings just weren't cooperating and that was frustrating as hell. As I leaned in closer to the mirror, trying to fix it, my reflection smiled.

I wasn't smiling.

my breath sucked in my throat. I jerked back so fast her chair stumbled, and I crashed to the floor.

Heart pounding, I somehow managed to get on my feet, staring at the mirror. my reflection stared back, wide-eyed and panicked, reflecting me.

"What just happened?" I whispered.

I grabbed my phone and snapped a quick photo of the mirror, hoping to catch whatever was going on. But when I checked the picture, it looked normal—just my reflection staring back.

No smile.

I let out a shaky laugh. *"Great. Now I'm officially losing my mind."*

I decided to call Ash. He was the only person I trusted to not call me crazy.

But Ash didn't answer. I left him a voicemail, trying to sound calm. *"Hey, it's me. Something weird is going on, something out of the box and I really need to talk to you. Call me back, once you're free, okay?"*

I hung up and jumped onto my bed, feeling exhausted. My phone buzzed a moment later, and my heart jumped. I grabbed it, thinking Ash had called back.

It wasn't Ash.

It was an airdrop request from Unknown Sender.

I hesitated, my finger hovering over the "Accept" button. I knew I probably shouldn't, but curiosity won this time. With a deep breath, and assuring myself that everything will be alright, I accepted the file.

A single photo appeared on my screen: a picture of me, sitting on my bed, staring at my phone.

my stomach sank as fast as something dropped from a certain hight.

I immediately got up, locking the door and pulling the curtains. My hands were trembling out of fear as I stared at the picture.

Someone had taken it. Someone was watching me.

I grabbed the journal, desperate for answers. I flipped through the pages, scanning the entries for anything that might explain what was happening. my eyes stopped on a line I hadn't noticed before:

"Don't trust the mirrors. They're not just reflections—they're windows. And they're watching."

My chest tightened. I slammed the journal shut and tossed it across the room.

"This isn't real," I said out loud. *"It can't be real."*

But I couldn't shake the feeling that it was.

That night, I avoided every mirror in the house. I brushed my teeth with my back to the bathroom mirror, covered the full-length mirror in my bedroom with a blanket, and even avoided looking at my phone screen for too long.

But the uneasiness followed me everywhere.

I was lying in bed, trying to read the journal again, when I felt it: a touch on the back of my neck, like someone was watching me, like someone just called me.

I sat straight, scanning the room. my eyes landed on the closet door, where the faded outline of my reflection was visible in the mirrored panel.

My reflection wasn't lying down.

It was standing, staring at me with its head tilted slightly to the side.

My throat went dry. I squeezed my eyes tightly, telling myself it wasn't real. It was just my imagination, nothing else.

I builds the courage and opened my eyes; the reflection was gone.

I let out a shaky breath, trying to calm myself down. That's when I noticed something new in the journal. On the inside cover, written in faded ink, were three words:

"Don't look away."

My stomach twisted.

My phone buzzed again.

Another airdrop request popped up on my screen. I didn't accept it this time, but the message preview still appeared.

It read:

"They see everything."

I threw my phone onto the nightstand, pulled the blanket over my head, and closed my eyes. For the first time since moving to Havenport, I didn't want to figure things out.

I just wanted to survive, just for now.

Chapter 6:

Glitch in the System

I wasn't exactly a hacker, but thanks to my side course I knew the basics, and stuff like that. curiousness can do anything to a person, and after what I experienced from the last few days, I was ready to do anything.

The abandoned building across the street had been giving me creepy vibes since day one. Its sealed windows and peeling paint were spooky enough, but it wasn't just the look of it—something didn't sit right. Like someone was observing from inside and when my phone kept catching up a random Wi-Fi signal labelled *"Omega_researches,"* I knew I need to check it out.

Sitting cross-legged on couch near the window with my laptop well-adjusted on a pillow, I legit gawked at screen.

"Okay, no big deal," I muttered to myself. *"I Just need to break into a Hella private Wi-Fi network. How hard can it be?"*

I opened my saviour which is YouTube, most of my hobbies were self-taught through YT, so the only way was to prompt *"how to hack Wi-Fi for beginners."* Ten minutes and a few of unclear tutorials later, I found a free software tool that looked simple enough.

I quickly downloaded it; my stomach was twisting from inside. The software started working, running lines of code across my screen like something out of a spy movie.

my heart pounded as fast as the program shook. After a few nervous minutes, a message popped up: ***Access Granted.***

"Holy crap," I whispered. I was satisfied with my job but wasn't sure if I should feel pleased or terrified.

What caught my eyes was same jagged circle which I was seeing everywhere. The network wasn't what I thought it would be. It wasn't full of boring files or random junk like I expected it. Instead, it was organized—too organized.

There were folders labelled:

Subjects

Surveillance Logs

Experiment Data

I was confused about everything, my eyes floated over the "Subjects" folder, my hand trembling. But I still clicked, and a long list of names appeared on the screen.

At first, they meant nothing to me. But as I scrolled, my stomach sank as deep as ocean.

Harper, Elleanor.

My name was there.

"What the actual hell," just to be sure I double checked

"Wait! What? Why is my name over here" saying it out loud I leaned closer to the screen.

I clicked on my name, and a file opened. Inside were records—detailed notes about my life. There were details of everything:

"Subject arrives in Havenport."

"Subject begins interacting with locals."

"Subject discovers journal."

my head spin as if everything is moving. Someone has been stalking my every move.

I backed out of the folder, my heart beat racing. I clicked on Surveillance record next.

There were hundreds of video files. Most were labelled with dates and locations I found—my house, the coffee shop, even the grocery store.

I clicked on one labelled Elleanor_Bedroom_12-20.

My own face came up straight on the screen. A photo of me sitting on my bed, scrolling through my phone, completely unaware that I was being recorded.

I smacked my laptop shut, the air seemed to vibrate with terror, my breathing was fragile. At first, I thought it might be some random stalker but that video...was something...

"This can't be real. This can't be real," I muttered, running my hands through hair.

But it was real. The files didn't just appear out of nowhere. Someone was inspecting me...closely.

But eventually, I opened the laptop and faced my fears. This time, I went to the *Experiment Data folder*.

The documents inside were modified, but I could still make out enough to get the gist.

Omega Code wasn't just any tech company. They were conducting research—researches on people. The files talked about *"social operation," "memory rebuilding,"* and something called *"Project Replication."*

I felt nauseas. I clicked on another file, and a diagram popped up. It showed a room filled with mirrors, like some kind of creepy funhouse. The caption underneath read:

"Reflections are the key to opening hidden memories."

"Oh my god!! it's all linked up as the journal mentioned" it clicked in the back of my mind.

My mind raced. The mirrors in my house. The delayed reflection. The weird messages in the journal. It all had to be connected.

I backed out of the folders and tried to dig deeper, but my screen suddenly went black.

"No, no, no," I whispered, rapidly tapping the keyboard. The laptop stayed dark for a moment before a message appeared in bold white text:

Unauthorized Access Detected.

My heart dropped.

Before I could react, my phone vibrated on the bed next to me. I picked it up, and a notification popped up on the screen:

"You shouldn't have done that."

I ogled at the message, my chest tightening like knot. I didn't recognize the number, but it didn't matter. Whoever sent it knew what I had just done.

my laptop restarted on its own, the screen blinking for a split second before going back to the normal desktop. The files were gone.

Every single one.

I paced my room, trying to figure out my next move. Someone—whoever was behind Omega Code—knew I had accessed the network. And if they'd been stalking me this whole time, they'd know exactly where I was.

I grabbed my bag and started packing. Clothes, the journal, my laptop—anything I thought I might need.

As I shoved my charger into the bag, my phone buzzed again.

This time, it was a video. I opened it, my hands trembling. The video was of me, standing in my room, staring at my laptop. It was taken from inside the closet mirror.

I dropped the phone like it was on fire, as if it burned me.

my mind was racing as I tried to solve the puzzle, trying to connect everything together. The journal's warnings, the files, the researches—it all pointed to one thing: I was part of some twisted experiment, and Omega Code wasn't going to let me walk away easily.

But I wasn't about to sit around and wait for whatever was coming.

Grabbing my bag, I threw it over my shoulder and headed for the door. I didn't know where I was going yet, but one thing was clear.

If Omega Code wanted to keep their secrets, they'd have to catch me first.

Chapter 7:

Ghosts of the Past

I didn't precisely feel safe roaming around Havenport anymore, and top of it Ash was not answering my calls, but I needed answers. my hunt led to the stranger that I met on the first day of Havenport

Apparently, she was Mrs. Clara Hartley, a permanent resident who apparently knew everyone and everything about the town. If anyone could link the dots up about the journal, Omega Code, and the creepy mirror trials, it would be only her.

Clara lived in a wrinkled old house on the edge of Havenport. The place looked as if straight out of a gothic horror movie, with vines crawling up the walls and an iron gate that creaked, the overall house looks like the house from *Courage of the cowardly dog cartoon*. I hesitated a bit before pushing it open.

I knocked on the door, which had a washed-out *"No request"* sign copied to it. For a moment, nothing happened, and I wondered if Clara was even home. Just as I was about to leave, the door opened a slightly.

"Yes?" came a voice, thin and wary.

"Hi, Mrs. Hartley? I'm Elleanor Harper, remember, I just moved here, and I was hoping to talk to you about..." I hesitated, wondering how to phrase it without sounding weird or unhinged. *"Something weird that's been happening in town."*

The door opened broader, revealing a small woman with sharp eyes that seemed to see right through me.

"You're the one who rented the old Bennett place, aren't you?" Clara asked, her voice sharper now.

I nodded, trying to hide my surprise. *"Yeah, that's me. You remember?"*

"Small town," Clara said with a shrug. *"Word gets around. Come in."*

The inside of Clara's house was messy but cosy. Souvenirs lined every existing space, and the air smelled softly of lavender and old books. Clara waved me to sit on a worn floral couch while she went to the kitchen.

When she returned, she was holding two mugs of tea. She handed one to me and sat down in an armchair across from mine.

"So, what's this about?" Clara asked, her tone curious but defended.

I took a deep breath and pulled the journal out of my bag. I settled it on the coffee table among them.

"I found this in the house," I said. *"It's... weird. The entries talk about shadows, unstable memories, stuff like that. And I think..."* I hesitated, then decided to just go for it. *"I assume it belonged to someone in your family?"* just a wild guess, maybe she would deny it and reveal something

Clara's face didn't change, but her knobs tightened around the mug. She gazed at the journal like it was something alive, something dangerous.

"Where exactly did you find this?" Clara asked, her voice low.

"In the attic. It was hidden under the planks," I replied. *"I think whoever wrote it knew something—something about the tests Omega Code has been doing."*

Clara didn't respond right away. She set her mug down, tilting back in her chair with a sigh.

"You've walked into something much bigger than you realize," she said finally.

Over the next hour, Clara told me everything.

So basically, the journal belonged to Clara's younger brother, Samuel. Back in the early 2000s, Havenport was still a sleepy casting town, but that changed when Omega Code set up shop. They claimed to be a tech company working on communication systems, but people in town had always suspected there was more to it.

Samuel was one of those people. He was curious to a responsibility, always digging where he didn't belong. He started noticing strange things happening around town—people acting out of character, memories that didn't add up, whispers of secret experiments.

Clara paused; her eyes distant. *"He tried to tell me about it, but I didn't take him seriously. I thought he was being paranoid."*

I leaned forward, hanging on every word. *"What happened to him?"*

"He vanished in blue," Clara said, her voice tight. *"One day, he told me he was close to finding proof—something that would blow the whole thing wide open. And then he was gone."*

"Gone like... moved away? Or...?" I trailed off, afraid to say what I was really thinking.

"Gone like vanished," Clara said flatly. *"No note, no goodbye. Just... gone. And the weirdest part? It's like people forgot he even existed. His friends stopped talking about him. Teachers acted like he'd never been in their classes. It was like someone wiped him out of everyone's memory."*

I felt a chill run down her spine.

Clara continued, explaining how Omega Code had deep roots in the town. They'd been experimenting on people for decades, using Havenport as a testing ground.

"Back then, it was more low-tech," Clara said. *"They didn't have all the fancy gadgets they have now, but the goal was the same—control. Manipulation. They wanted to see how far they could push people before they broke."*

My mind raced. *"And the mirrors? The journals talk about mirrors being windows or something."*

Clara nodded grimly. *"Samuel thought they were using reflections to mess with people's minds. He said it wasn't just about what you saw—it was about what they wanted you to see. He was convinced the mirrors were some kind of surveillance tool."*

My body shivered, remembering my own experiences with the mirrors in my house, correction the Bennett house.

"What about Omega Code now?" I asked. *"Are they still... doing this?"*

Clara hesitated, then nodded. *"They've gotten smarter about it. More subtle. Most people don't even realize they're part of the experiment. But if you've found this journal, and you're seeing the signs, it means they've marked you."*

"Marked me for what?" I asked, my voice shaking.

"I don't know," Clara admitted. *"But if they're watching you, it's not good. You need to be careful."*

I clenched my fists, anger rising in my chest. *"I'm not just going to sit around and let them mess with me. There has to be a way to stop this."*

Clara gave me a sad smile. *"That's what Samuel thought, too."*

When I left Clara's house, the sun was starting to set, casting long shadows across the street. My mind was buzzing with everything Clara said.

Samuel's disappearance, the experiments, the mirrors—it all linked back to Omega Code. And now, I was part of it.

But unlike Samuel, I wasn't going to vanish quietly.

I was going to fight back.

Even if it meant putting everything on the line.

Chapter 8:

Trust No One

I was already on edge, but the paranoia hit on a next level when even the people I thought I could trust started acting... off.

It started with Ash. He hadn't picked my calls in days, which wasn't unusual for him—he'd always been the type to "accidentally" ghost people. But this felt different. He didn't even read my texts, which was very not-Ash would do. Normally, he'd at least send a "lol busy" or a meme in response.

I started at my phone, debating whether to try calling him again. Finally, I gave in, dialling his number and holding my breath.

The call went straight to voicemail.

"Hey, it's me again," I said, trying to keep my voice steady. *"Look, I know I maybe sound crazy, but I really need to talk to you. I think... I think something's happening. And I don't know who else to turn up."*

I hung up, tossing my phone on bed.

I miss Mia, at least she wouldn't ghost me like this.

I haven't heard anything about her. No updates, no news, no one even seemed to care. It was like Mia had never existed, which only added to my growing list of things that didn't make sense.

I tried bringing it up to the other baristas at the café where Mia had worked, but they just gave me blank stares.

"Mia?" one of them said, furrowing their brow. *"Sorry, I don't know who that is."*

"You know—Mia," I pressed. *"Short, colourful hair, always wore those chunky earrings. She worked here last week!"*

The barista just shook their head, looking at me like I was the one who'd lost it.

"Sorry, we haven't had anyone like that working here," they said before turning away to clean the counter.

I felt like I was going to scream.

The final straw came when the anonymous account started posting again.

The first post was just a photo: a shot of the Havenport lighthouse, taken at sunset. Harmless enough, except for one thing—it was the exact photo I had taken on my first day in town.

My stomach flipped as I stared at the post. There was no way anyone else could've taken that picture. The angle, the lighting—it was mine.

I checked the account's bio again, hoping for some clue about who was behind it. Nothing. Just the same mysterious tagline: *"Everything is connected."*

The next post came a few hours later. This time, it was a riddle:

"What can see without eyes, hear without ears, and remember without a mind?"

I frowned, rereading the words again and again. It felt familiar, like something I'd heard before. I grabbed the journal from the nightstand and flipped over the pages, searching for whatsoever that might explain the riddle.

Halfway through, she found it.

The answer was written in Samuel's shaky handwriting: ***"A system."***

My hands were legit trembling as I ogled at the journal. A system? Was that what Omega Code was building? A system that could watch, listen, and manipulate people without them even knowing?

My phone buzzed with a notification, making me jump. It was another post from the account—a photo of my house, taken from the street.

I felt the blood drain from her entire body.

I grabbed my phone as quickly as I could and locked all the doors and windows, my mind racing. Was someone stalking me? Following me?

My phone buzzed again.

This time, it was a direct message.

"Do you trust them?"

I stared at the screen, my fingers hovering over the keyboard. I didn't know who *"them"* was supposed to be, but I was pretty sure the answer was no.

"Who are you?" I typed back, my heart pounding.

The reply came almost instantly: ***"Someone who knows what you've seen."***

I couldn't sleep that night. I stayed up all night, scrolling through the account's posts and covering together what little I could.

The riddles, the photos—they weren't any random stuff. They were clues, breadcrumbs leading me toward something. But what?

By morning, I wasn't closer to an answer, but one thing was clear: I couldn't trust anyone, not even myself.

Especially not myself.

I remembered the journal's warning: ***"Never trust what feels real."***

My phone buzzed with one last message before the account went silent:

"Be careful who you turn to. They're not who they seem."

I put my phone down, my hands shaking.

I was officially on my own.

Chapter 9:

The Game Begins

I was sitting on my couch, Sketching random stuff. When a random number which was blocked, but after everything I'd been through, I wasn't surprised.

I let it ring once, twice, three times, debating or fighting my mind whether to answer. At the end of course my curiosity won.

"Hello?" I said, trying to keep my voice steady.

"Elleanor Harper," a calm, professional voice replied. *"We've been trying to reach you."*

My abdominal roiled. *"Who is this?"*

The voice didn't hesitate. *"We represent Omega Code. We understand you've been looking into matters that don't concern you."*

I sat up straight, my pulse spiking. "*You've got to be kidding me."*

"We'd like to offer you an opportunity," the voice continued, completely unfazed by my reaction. *"A chance to walk away from all of this—no harm, no foul. In fact, we're prepared to compensate you generously for your cooperation."*

I barked out a laugh, though there was no humour in it. "*Compensate me? You think I care about money?"*

"Huh! Cliché" a voice came back in my mind, it is a curious phenomenon that when a person feels absurd in the empire of intellectual, they seek relief in the physical empire of wealth as if riches could pay off everything even, if they could they wouldn't buy any intelligence.

"You might, once you hear the amount," the voice said smoothly.

A text notification popped up on my screen. It was a bank transfer screenshot showing six figures—enough to cover my rent for years, pay off my student loans, and still have cash left over.

"Take the offer, Ms. Harper," the voice said. *"You can leave Havenport, start fresh somewhere else. Forget all of this ever happened."*

My jaw clenched at one point it hurt. *"Yeah, no thanks. Keep your blood money."*

The line went silent for a moment, and for a second, I thought they'd hung up. Then the voice spoke again, colder this time.

"Are you sure that's the choice you want to make?"

Sure, as hell.

I walked into the coffee shop, desperate for caffeine after another sleepless night. The barista—a different one this time, since Mia had vanished—looked up and froze.

"Oh," they said, their tone icy. *"It's you."*

I blinked. *"Uh, yeah? Can I just get a coffee?"*

The barista didn't move. *"You shouldn't be here."*

"What's that supposed to mean?" I asked, confused and a little irritated.

But the barista just shook their head, muttering something underneath her breath before turning to make my drink.

When I got my coffee, the cup had a single word scrawled on it: *Trouble.*

I tried brushing it off as a weird coincidence, but as the day went on, the atmosphere in town got worse.

People stared at me as I walked down the street, their whispers following me wherever I went.

"That's her."

"Crazy, isn't she?"

"Thought she left already."

I gritted my teeth so hard that maybe I would have chipped a tooth, fighting the urge to yell at them. I didn't know how Omega had done it, but it was clear they'd turned the entire town against me.

By evening, the full scope of their plan became clear.

my landlord Bannet showed up at my door apparently his, he looked apologetic but firm. *"Look, Elleanor,"* he said, avoiding my eyes, *"you've been a great tenant, but I'm gonna need you to move out. There've been... complaints."*

"Complaints about what?" I demanded.

He scratched the back of his neck, clearly uncomfortable. *"People are saying you've been acting unstable. Causing trouble around town."*

I stared at him, dumbfounded. *"Are you serious right now? You've known me for months! You know that's not true."*

He sighed. *"I'm sorry, Elleanor. I really am. But I've got other tenants to think about. You've got until the end of the week."*

That night, I sat in a darkened living room, feeling the walls close in. I scrolled through social media, watching *Netflix* hoping for a distraction, but what I found was worse.

my face was everywhere. Posts accusing me of everything from sabotage to harassment flooded the town's community pages. Photos of me looking angry or dishevelled—probably taken without my knowledge—were plastered alongside captions like *"Is she dangerous?"* and *"Why hasn't she been arrested yet?"*

its not shocking cause Ai could possibly can do anything other than feeling emotions and household chores.

I threw my phone onto the couch, my hands shaking.

This was Omega's game. They were trying to isolate me, make me look like the villain so no one would believe me.

But the worst part came when I checked my emails.

There, in my inbox, was a message with the subject line: ***Proof***.

I hesitated before opening it. Inside was a single image—mine, standing in front of the coffee shop, spray paint in hand, tagging the window with one of the symbols from the journal.

I stared at the photo, my heart sinking.

I hadn't done that.

I knew I hadn't.

But the picture was so clear, so perfect, it would be impossible to convince anyone otherwise.

By the time morning rolled around, I was done playing defence.

Putting my ego aside, I grabbed my phone and called Ash again, not even caring that he ghost's each and every time but I didn't have any other option left, maybe I will regret calling or again be disappointed when he doesn't pick up, but one last try won't kill anyone, right!?

This time, he picked up.

"Ellie?" he said, his voice groggy. *"What's going on?"*

"I need your help," I said, cutting straight to the point. *"omega's coming after me. They're trying to ruin my life, and I can't fight them alone."*

There was a pause on the other end of the line.

"Ash?" I prompted, my heart sinking.

"I don't know, Ellie," he said finally. *"You've been acting kinda... different lately. Maybe they're not wrong."*

My stomach dropped. *"Are you kidding me right now?"*

"I'm just saying," he continued, *"maybe you need to take a step back. Clear your head..."*

I was done, I hung up before he can complete, my hands trembling with anger.

Yeah, I regrate calling him, I was too stunned to react, perhaps I trusted the wrong person

Fine. If no one else was going to help me, I'd figure this out on my own.

I grabbed the journal from nightstand, flipping over the pages until I found what I was looking for: *a list of addresses scribbled in the margins.*

If Omega wanted to play games, I'd beat them at their own. It was time to go deeper into their world—no matter what.

Chapter 10: Memories Unravelled

Memories fade away from my mind

But in my heart, they're left behind

My heart remembers.

I sat cross-legged on bed; the journal spread out in front of me. The attic window let in just enough moonlight to spooky shadows across the pages. I scanned through the worn boundaries until I found the part I couldn't stop rereading—a passage about rooted memories.

"Memories are the strings they use to control you. Pull one wrong move, and you'll unravel."

The words made my stomach roil. Memories had always been special to me, the one thing that kept me grounded. My mom's laugh when I dropped paint as a kid. That one summer I spent playing Legos with my dad. The night I cried over a boy, and my best friend told me, I deserved better.

But now, I wasn't uncertain any of that was real.

The first real clash in my memories came earlier that day when I tried to call my mom. The number rang out, ultimately going to voicemail, but the speech on the recording wasn't my mom's. It was some random stranger's, saying a totally different name.

"Hey, you've reached Debra. Leave a message!"

I froze. I double-checked just to be sure, but it was the same one I'd been calling for years.

I left a message anyway, my voice shaky. *"Uh, Mom? It's me, Ellie. I think there's something weird going on. Can you call me back?"* saying this a tear rolled up my cheeks, this could be the first spell I cried after stepping in Havenport

When I hung up, an unaware unease settled in my chest.

Later, in the journal, I found a page with comprehensive advices on accessing Omega's secret memory files. It was risky, but I was way past caring about risks. I hacked into their network again, fingers flying over the keyboard in my dimly lit room.

After a few failed passwords, I cracked it somehow.

The files were labelled Subjects*: **Memory Mapping.***

My eyes scanned the page, heart racing as I found my name. Elleanor Harper. Subject #1485. I clicked on it, and a document popped up.

The first line made my breath hitch.

"Childhood memory sequence began: untrue."

my eyes dashed to the details, each word hitting me like a punch to the gut. *The journal entry about a treehouse? Fake. my parents' constant support? Composed. Even the memory of my best friend consoling me was a "positive support insert."*

My chest felt tight.

"No. This can't be right," I mumbled.

I dug deeper, discovering files labelled *"Behavioural Challenging"* and *"Personality Correction."* my blood ran cold as I saw timestamps that corresponded to major life events.

The breakup I'd thought was earth-crushing? Written to test my flexibility.

My decision to move to Havenport? Encouraged by a hidden program to keep me within Omega's reach.

My entire life was a lie.

That night, sleep wasn't an option. I sat with the journal in my lap, flipping over it as if the writer might somehow answer the question that kept twisting in my head:

If my memories aren't mine, then who am I?

Ash called while I was pacing around, but I ignored it. I didn't know how to explain any of this to him. Heck, I couldn't even explain it to myself and after what he said earlier....

But Ash wasn't the type to let me ghost him. Twenty minutes later, there was a knock at my door.

When I let him in, I didn't even try to hide the tears flowing down my face. I was facing too many emotions at the same time, I totally forgot what Ash did.

"I'm losing my mind, I just don't want to talk to you Ash," I said, my voice barely above a whisper.

"Look, Ells, I'm sorry for earlier. It's just..." Ash trailed off, running a hand through his messy hair. His jaw clenched as if the words physically hurt to say. *"I just want to keep you safe. This whole Omega thing—it's crazy dangerous. And I can't...I won't lose you. You're the only person who doesn't treat me like I'm some kind of...legend or whatever."*

I crossed my arms, my voice sharp. *"That's your excuse for acting like a total jerk? It doesn't justify how you treated me, Ash."*

He sighed, his shoulders slumping in defeat. *"I know, I know. I shouldn't have said, what I did. It was messed up, and I hate myself for it."* He paused, his voice softening. *"But...I was trying to protect you. If Omega finds out you have someone backing you up, they'll only come harder for you. I thought distancing myself was the only way to keep you safe, even if it meant..."* His voice cracked slightly, but he quickly swallowed it down. *"Even if it meant you hated me."*

I blinked at him, trying to process his words. *"And how do you even know so much about Omega?"*

Ash's face hardened, his jaw tightening as his gaze dropped to the floor. *"I think it's time you finally get some answers,"* he said quietly, his voice almost too calm, like he was steeling himself for something painful.

He took a shaky breath before continuing. *"I was sixteen when I lost my baby sister. She was twelve. She was the best, you know? Always following me around, making me laugh when I didn't want to."* He smiled faintly at the memory, but it vanished as quickly as it came. *"One day, she met this girl from Bennett House, and they became friends. The girl...she was different. She would talk about these wild things—mirrors, voices, shadows that moved when no one else could see them. Paranormal-type stuff. My sister was so curious, so into it."*

I didn't say anything, sensing he needed to get it all out.

Ash's voice grew heavier. *"I told her to stop listening to that nonsense. I told her it was just stories. But she didn't listen. She told me—God, I still hear her voice sometimes—she told me, 'Ash, it's real. The mirrors, the voices, everything. We're gonna figure it out.'"* He stopped, his throat working as he fought back the emotion rising in his voice. *"Then one day...she was gone. Just like that. Disappeared without a trace. I know now that Omega took her, just like they took Mia."*

His words hit me like a punch to the gut. My throat tightened, and guilt clawed at my chest. If it weren't for me dragging Mia into this, she'd still be here. I tried to hold back my tears, but they burned hot in my eyes, threatening to spill.

Ash's voice softened, almost breaking. *"That's why I tried to warn you when we first met. I didn't want you to end up like her. But I failed. I couldn't stop Mia from being taken, and it's killing me."*

I wiped at my face quickly, trying to pull myself together. *"Ash, I—"*

He cut me off, his voice steadier now. *"After I lost her, I became obsessed with finding out the truth. That's when I started uncovering all of this—Omega, the experiments, everything. And somewhere along the way...I found out about you, Ellie."*

I froze is there something I am missing out? *"What do you mean?"*

Ash hesitated, then looked me dead in the eye. "Ells, you're not just caught in this—you're part of it. You're a subject. They've been watching you for years, controlling things around you. That's why I backed off. I thought if I stayed away, maybe we could stay under their radar for just a little longer."

"I already knew this Ash, I hacked their Wi-Fi and..."

"Tell me, what did you find?" Ash glanced at the open laptop and the journal, mending together enough to know this was about Omega.

I hesitated, and then gave in, *"Everything I know about my life—it's fake. My memories, my personality, everything. They built me, Ash. I'm not even real."*

Ash frowned, stepping closer. *"That's not true, Ells. You're real to me."*

His words were meant to comfort me, but they only made me angrier.

"You don't get it!" I snapped. *"They've been controlling me my whole life. Every choice, every sentiment. Even us—what if this isn't*

real either? What if they made me feel this way about you?"

The room fell silent.

Ash looked at me, his expression softer than I'd ever seen it. *"Ellie, you're not just a subject of memories. You're more than that. Possibly they messed this up with your past, but they can't switch what you do now. That's all you."*

Ash's words didn't magically fix everything, but they gave I rather to hold on something. I spent the rest of the night sifting through files and patching together remains of my real past.

I found hints of a life that was mine before Omega intervened—a birthday party I didn't recognize, a childhood home in a town I'd never been to. It wasn't much, but it was a start.

By morning, I wasn't okay, but I wasn't broken either. I am not a crystal ball that could be broken easily.

For the first time in weeks, I felt like I had a purpose.

Omega had taken my memories, my identity.

But I was going to get them back, at any cost.

Chapter 11:

The Heart of the Lie

My heart pounded hard enough that it seemed ready to leap from my chest. I squatted in the shadows of the underground parking garage owned by Omega Code, gripping a stolen ID badge with sweaty palm.

Breaking into Omega's headquarters hadn't been easy. I had spent weeks plotting out their security patterns, studying employee activities, and hacking into their systems to create a fake identity. But even with all my prep, the place was more heartened than a billionaire's mansion.

The ID badge had been my golden ticket—or so I hoped.

The process of entering the building slid past with surprizing ease. I swiped the badge at the side entrance and was holding my breath as the light in the scanner went green.

"Okay, step one done," I whispered to myself, glancing around the empty hall.

Inside, it was just like I imagined—cold, antiseptic, and far too high-tech. The walls were metallic, the floors glowed oddly, and every corner appeared to have a camera or a motion sensor. I pulled the hoodie tighter over my head, trying to look like I belonged there, but every step felt like a countdown to getting caught.

My earbuds buzzed, and Ash's voice came as a whisper.

"You good?"

tapped the mic clipped to my collar. *"So far, yeah. This place is insane, though. It's like Silicon Valley threw up in here."*

"Focus," Ash said, his voice firm but tinged with concern. *"You know what you're looking for."*

I nodded, even though he couldn't see me. *"Yeah. The server room."*

Locating the server room hadn't been the problem—that was getting in. This door had a keypad, scanner, and a card reader.

"Calm down, Ellie you have solved many puzzles in your life, oh! Wait, they might not be my actual memory," I mutter with spite sarcasm, pulling out small device Mia had arranged me before disappearing. This thing looks like a really nasty, heavy piece USB key; when I plug it in to the keypad, a flood of numbers starts ejecting out on its tiny screen

"C'mon, c'mon," I mumbled, glancing sideways over my shoulder.

Finally, after what looked like an eternity, the keypad beeped, and the door was unlocked.

I slipped inside, letting out a shaky breath.

The room was huge, occupied with gigantic racks of servers that buzzed dimly. Screens displayed data system that running too fast for me to follow. It felt like stepping into the brain of a living machine.

I found a device to plugged in my own flash drive, my only purpose being to extract the files I needed.

"Okay, Ash, I reached," I said, my fingers hovering over the keyboard.

The flash drive started downloading files, and I watched as folder after folder filled the screen:

Subject Profiles

Memory Grafting Reports

Behavioural Test Results

Her vision blurred when she saw familiar names:

Subject #1485: Elleanor Harper.

Subject #1426: Ash Cooper.

Subject: #2015: Mia Bloom.

I hesitated, then opened the file which had my name.

The first thing I saw was a picture of myself—barely ten years old, sitting in a sterile white room. I looked confused, scared. Notes underneath described me as "highly interested" and "ideal for early-stage trials."

I scrolled down, my eyes widening as I read:

Memory Wipe: Complete.

Behavioural Conditioning: Ongoing.

Emotional Adjustment: Successful.

My throat tightened. They'd been playing with me since I was a child, peeling away all I knew and putting in this fucking system. what? A life that wasn't mine? A personality that was controlled?

I opened a video file called Adjustment Test 1.

The screen came to life with footage of mine at the fourteen, sitting in what appeared to be a school classroom. A voice off-camera asked me questions.

"What makes you happy, Ellie?

"Spending time with my friends," I replied.

"And what would you do if you couldn't see them anymore?"

I replied all the question as if I was bot or something, or perhaps hypnotised

My fourteen-year-old self-paused, then gave a cold smile lightly. *"I'd find new ones."*

The voice resumed, steady and technical. *"Good. And what if someone hurt them?"*

my face went blank. *"I'd stop them."*

I banged the laptop closed, my stomach roiling, I didn't know how to feel after watching the footage, many emotions were running in my heart.

As the file finishes its download, I went digging over the other files, digging into the core of Omega's experiment.

They weren't just reworking memories-they were training people. They were creating control over them, obedient versions of themselves. I wasn't the only one. There were hundreds of names listed, each with a profile detailing how Omega had manipulated their lives.

This was not about technology. It was about power.

Omega was using their AI to mould people into whatever they needed-the so-called loyal workers, compliant citizens, even hostages in larger systems.

And I had been one of their "success stories."

Something clanked loudly in my line of hearing.

Footsteps.

I snatched the flash drive from the device and threw it in my pocket. My heart racing, the server room door slid open.

A man in a suit entered, sharp eyes scrubbing the space.

"Is someone there?"

I bent behind the rack of servers and held my breath; one wrong move and I am done.

The man crept closer, and my head spun. I could not let them catch me not now when I this close to find the truth, not when I finally had what I needed as proof.

Just as the man hit the corner, I grabbed a nearby fire extinguisher and swung it full force, knocking the guy down.

"Sorry, dude, it's not my fault" I muttered, stepping over him.

"Ash," I breathed into the earpiece. *"You need to get me out of here, right. Now."* Ash said sounding scared

"I know," I whispered as I rushed back into the hallway.

The building was a maze, and I was always the smart one when it comes to puzzles.

Alarms began to blast and red lights flashed overhead, but I ran, holding the flash drive as if my life depended on it.

It did actually.

I burst out into the cool night air, shaking. Ash waited in a car nearby, and I settled myself into the passenger seat, banging the door shut.

"Drive!" I screamed, my voice cracking. Ash didn't say a word. He stunned it, and they darned out of the Omega headquarters, the lights of the city blurring around us.

I sat back in my seat, my hand grasping the flash drive like it was a weapon to save the world.

"They have been controlling me," I said, my voice hollow. *"My whole life. And not just me. Hundreds of them."*

I didn't reveal that Ash name was there in the subjects, I didn't feel to mention it...it might not be the perfect time to reveal, he was already carrying so much and this truth would shatter him. For now, I'd keep it to myself, waiting for the moment when it destroys what little strength he had.

Ash cast a look over at me, his jaw set hard. *"Then we have to take them down."*

For the first time that evening, I allowed myself a tiny, firm smile.

"Yeah," I said. *"We will."*

Chapter 12:

A Choice to Make

Choices we make, a story they tell

I sat on the floor of Ash's apartment, surrounded by printouts, files, and my laptop. The flash drive I stole from Omega Code was plugged in, its blue light blinking like it was mocking me. I stared at the screen; my chest tight with anxiety.

The files show everything—the lies, the manipulation, the experiments. Every secret Omega had worked so hard to bury was now in my hands.

But the weight of it was crushing me from inside.

"What do I even do with this?" I muttered frustrated, running a hand through my hair.

Ash, sitting across from me, leaned back against the couch, his arms crossed. His face was serious, his usual smirk replaced by something softer, more thoughtful.

"You know what you have to do," he said, his voice steady. *"Expose them."*

I shot him a look. *"It's not that simple, Ash. If I do that, they'll come after me. Hard. They'll come after you too."*

"Let them," he said, without hesitation. *"I'm not scared of them."*

I let out a bitter laugh. *"That's easy for you to say. Your entire life hasn't been some... science experiment."* Deep down I know it's a lie.

Omega can control my memories, but not what my heart says.

Ash moved closer, his expression softening. *"Ellie, your life isn't just what they made it. It's what you've done with it. The choices you've made, the people you've helped—that's all you. Not them."*

Ash is right! Choices,

Choices tells a person's true personality on the other hand I wonder how will Ash react after knowing the truth. But his words hung in the air, heavy but comforting.

I sighed, picking up one of the printouts. It was a list of other *"subjects,"* people like me who had been manipulated by Omega. Some of the names were crossed out, with notes that read Failed Experiment or Unresponsive.

I felt a wave of nausea. *"I don't even know if these people are alive. What if I expose this and it doesn't help anyone? What if it just gets worse?"*

Ash reached over me, grabbing the paper from my hands. *"And what if it doesn't? What if you save someone, Ells? What if you save yourself?"*

I looked at him, my eyes hurtful. *"Why do you care so much? I'm just some messed-up science project."*

Ash shook his head, his gaze locking with mine. *"You're not just anything, Ellie. You're... you. And I care because I see you fighting every day, even when you don't think you can win. That's worth caring about."*

His words made my chest ache, but in a good way. I hadn't realized how much I needed someone to say that—to remind her that I was more than what Omega had done to me.

I blinked back tears, nodding. *"Okay. But if we do this, we need a plan. A good one. Because I'm not going down without a fight."*

Ash grinned, the tension in the room easing slightly. *"That's the Ellie I know."*

His smile gave me a hope.

The next few hours were a blur of planning and arguing. I wanted to leak the files anonymously, but Ash insisted they needed to do more than just drop the information online.

"They'll bury it if we don't make noise," he said. *"We need to hit them where it hurts."*

"And where's that?"

Ash smirked. *"Their reputation. Companies like Omega bloom on trust. If people stop believing in them, they crumble."*

I hated how right he was.

"I hate to admit but you are indeed a smartass"

Ash smile grew wider that gave me the feeling I never felt before,

By the time the sun started rising, they had a plan: I would release the files to multiple news outlets, while Ash worked on coordinating with a few hackers he knew to take down Omega's website. It wasn't perfect, but it was something.

But as they packed up their gear, I couldn't shake the feeling that I was missing something.

"What if it's not enough?" I asked, my voice barely above a whisper.

Ash placed a hand on my shoulder, squeezing gently. *"It's enough because it's you. You're enough, Ells."*

My throat tightened, and I turned away, trying to hide how much his words meant.

The final step was the hardest.

I sat at across my laptop, my finger hovering over the "Send" button. The files were ready to go, the emails already drafted.

This was it. Once I hit send, there was no going back.

I glanced at Ash, who was watching me closely. *"What if I'm making a mistake?"*

"You're not," he said firmly. *"You're doing just the right thing."*

I nodded, taking a deep breath.

And then finally clicked it.

The moment the emails sent, I felt a strange mix of relief and fear.

"It's done," I said, leaning back in my chair.

Ash smiled, but it didn't quite reach his eyes. *"You're a badass, Harper."*

I laughed, even as tears streamed down my face. But our moment of triumph didn't last long. Within minutes, my phone buzzed with an incoming call. I didn't recognize the number, but I had a pretty good idea who it was.

"Don't answer it," Ash warned.

I ignored him, picking up the call.

A smooth, detached voice came through the line. *"You've made a very big mistake, Ms. Harper."*

My grip on the phone tightened. *"No, I think I finally did something right."*

There was a pause, then a low chuckle. *"You think this is over? You've only just begun to understand how deep this goes."*

The call ended, leaving me shaking.

Ash pulled me into a hug, his arms strong and reassuring. *"They're bluffing. We'll handle whatever comes next."*

For the first time in a long time, I believed him.

As the news began to spread and Omega's secrets were exposed, me and Ash knew our fight wasn't over.

But for now, we had each other.

And that was enough.

Chapter 13:

The Connection

Ash has been acting weird lately, like avoiding eye contacts, answering straight to the point, not talking much, the only topic which we talked about was Omega rather he is avoiding my text, it seemed as if Ash is avoiding working with me

Ash had booked a motel cause even his apartment wasn't safe enough to hang around.

I sat cross-legged on the bed in the dimly lit motel room, arms crossed and glaring at Ash. He was hanging around, his back was half-turned to me, staring out into the parking lot as if the answers to all their problems were written on the crack of the window.

"You've been acting weird lately," I broke the silence.

Ash didn't answer, his fingers tapping on the window.

"I'm serious," I pushed, my tone sharper now. *"One second, you're acting like we're this unbreakable team, and the next, you're all moody and distant. What's going on?"*

Ash sighed, his shoulders falling. *"Ellie, it's not the time for this."*

"Oh, it's exactly the time," I shot back, sitting up straighter. *"Because if we're going to take down Omega or figure out what's happening with this journal, we need to be on the same page. And right now, you're acting like you're reading a completely different book."*

That got his attention. Ash turned to me; his face shadowed but his eyes stormy. *"You don't get it,"* he said quietly, his voice barely above a whisper.

I tilted my head, my frustration rising. *"Then make me get it, Ash. You're supposed to have my back, remember? But lately, it feels like you're just...."*

Ash pushed off the windows and paced the room, running a hand through his hair. *"It's not that simple, Ellie."*

"Nothing about this is simple," I opposed, standing now. *"But we're in this together. At least, I thought we were."*

He stopped, his hands on his hips as he looked at me. *"You don't think I have your back? Ells, I've been pulling every string, taking every risk, just to keep you safe."*

I narrowed my eyes. *"Safe from what? From Omega? From the experiments? Newsflash, Ash, I'm already knee-deep in this mess. You keeping secrets isn't going to change that."*

"That's the problem!" he snapped, his voice rising. *"You're already in this, and it's dangerous. And if I'm not careful, it's going to get you hurt."*

I took a step closer, my voice softer but no less determined. *"So what? You just decide to pull away? Shut me out? That's not how this works, Ash."*

He stared at me; his jaw tight. *"You think it's easy for me? Watching you risk your life every day, knowing there's nothing I can do to stop it?"*

"Then why don't you just say that?" I asked, my tone laced with exasperation. *"Why not just talk to me instead of shutting me out?"*

Ash shook his head, letting out a bitter laugh. *"Because talking doesn't fix anything. It doesn't change the fact that you're stubborn and reckless and... God, Ellie, you don't even realize how much you mean to me, do you?"*

I froze, my breath catching. *"What are you saying?"*

He stepped closer, the space between us shrinking to almost nothing. *"I'm saying that you drive me crazy. That I can't stop thinking about you. That every time you put yourself in danger, it feels like my world's about to collapse."*

my heart was pounding now, and I wasn't sure if it was from his words or the way he was looking at me—like I was the only thing keeping him grounded.

"Ash..." I began, but he cut me off.

"No, let me finish," he said, his voice softer now. *"I've been pulling away because I'm scared. Scared that if I let myself care too much, I won't be able to do what needs to be done. And I can't afford to lose you, Ells. Not you."*

The room was silent, the weight of his confession hanging heavy in the air. I don't know what to say. Part of me wanted to yell at him for being so frustrating, for making me feel things I wasn't ready to deal with. But another part of me—maybe the bigger part—wanted to grab him by the collar and kiss him until the rest of the world vanishes away.

"I don't know what to say to that," I admitted finally, my voice barely above a whisper.

Ash looked away, a hint of regret curling across his face. *"You don't have to say anything. I just... I needed you to know."*

I nodded slowly, my emotions a tangled mess.

"Okay. But Ash?"

"Yeah?"

I stepped closer, my gaze steady. *"Don't ever shut me out again. We're in this together, no matter how messy it gets."*

He smiled faintly, the tension in his shoulders easing slightly. *"Deal."*

The moment remained between us, charged with an energy neither of us knew how to handle. But the sound of a car pulling into the parking lot broke the spell, reminding them of the mission still ahead.

"We should leave," Ash said, his voice back to its usual calm.

I nodded, grabbing my bag. But as we headed for the door, I couldn't help but look at him, my mind racing with thoughts I wasn't ready to confront.

Maybe there wasn't time for love in the middle of a mission. But that didn't mean it wasn't there, quietly growing in the spaces between us shared fears and whispered truths.

Chapter 14: Unseen Threads

The dim glow of my laptop screen shadows across the walls of the safe house. me and Ash sat side by side, bent over as we inspected over the encrypted files that Ash had stolen during a risky solo mission. The tension between us was intense, a blend of frustration, purpose, and something neither of us dared name.

"I don't get it," I muttered, scrolling through lines of code. *"These files—there's something missing. It's like Omega's intentionally left gaps, like they want us to find this but not really understand it."*

Ash leaned closer, furrowing his eyebrow as he analysed the screen. *"It's bait,"* he said finally. *"They're trying to push us into a trap."*

I glanced at him; the sharp angle of his jaw lit by the screen's bluish light. *"Then why take the risk to grab these files in the first place?"*

Ash met my gaze, his voice quiet but steady. *"Because every piece of the puzzle is important. And because you deserve answers."*

My stomach flipped, and I looked away, focusing on the screen. *"You say that like you're not part of this too."*

The room fell into an uneasy silence, broken only by the buzz of the laptop. My thoughts were a tornado of questions I was too afraid to ask. Why did Ash care so much? Why did his words always carry this weight, like they meant more than he was willing to admit?

Finally, I broke the silence. *"You're still not telling me everything, are you?"*

Ash stiffened but didn't respond immediately. When he did, his voice was heavy with hesitation. *"There are some things I'm not proud of, Ellie. Things I don't know how to explain yet."*

"That's not fair," I said, my frustration bubbling over. I turned to face him fully. *"You can't just keep me in the dark and expect me to trust you."*

Ash ran a hand through his hair, his expression conflicted. *"I'm not trying to keep you in the dark. I just—"* He exhaled sharply. *"I'm trying to protect you."*

"Protect me from what, Ash, from Omega, from the truth? Or from yourself" I scoffed, crossing my arms. *"You keep saying that, but I'm starting to think it's just an excuse."*

His eyes flashed with a mixture of anger and something else—something raw and thoughtless. *"From losing you,"* he said, his voice barely above a whisper.

I blinked, my breath catching in my throat. *"Ash..."*

He looked away, the helplessness in his expression quickly masked. *"Forget it. We should focus on the files."*

But I wasn't ready to let it go. My reached out, my hand brushing his. *"No. You don't get to drop a bomb like that and then act like it doesn't matter."*

Ash's shoulders tensed, and for a minute, I thought he might shut me out again. But then he turned back to me, his gaze intense. *"It does matter. More than you realize. But if I let it matter too much—if I let myself feel—then I might not be able to do what needs to be done."*

I swallowed hard, my chest tightening. *"You don't have to do this alone, Ash. Whatever you're carrying, we can handle it together. Isn't that the whole point of us being a team?"*

Ash stared at me for what felt like an eternity, his internal battle playing out in the flicker of his eyes. Finally, he nodded, a faint, almost faint movement. *"You're right,"* he said softly. *"But it's not easy for me. Letting people in—it's never been easy."*

I smiled faintly, my frustration melting into something warmer. *"Well, lucky for you, I'm stubborn. You're stuck with me, whether you like it or not."*

Ash chuckled, the sound low and rough, but it eased the tension between us. *"I think I like it."*

Our eyes met, and for a second, the world outside the safe house didn't exist. It was just us, two people directing a mess of plots and secrets while trying to hold onto something real.

Before either of them could say more, my laptop struck, signalling that the decoding process was complete. The moment crushed, and we turned back to the screen, our focus moving to the task.

But as we worked side by side, our shoulders brushing occasionally, I couldn't help but feel that something had changed between us. A thread had been pulled, separating the walls Ash had built around himself. And though we hadn't said it utter, I knew we were beginning to see each other in a different light—one that made the risks of our mission feel even higher.

They had a long way to go, and the road ahead would be dangerous. But for the first time, I felt like we might actually make it out of this—together.

Chapter 15:

The Reckoning

They can control minds but not hearts.

Ash stood frozen in the dimly lit room, the glow of the computer screen casting shadows across his face. The words on the screen swirled together, each line of code a punch to the gut. His name. His designation. His file.

He scrolled down, his hands shaking, barely able to keep his eyes on the screen. Experiment #1426. Subject Status: Active. Purpose: Behavioural Response and Emotional Integration Test. His entire life, reduced to clinical bullet points and cold, detached observations.

"Test successful. Subject displays high emotional adaptability and protective instincts."

"What the hell is this?" Ash muttered, his voice cracking. His breathing quickened, his chest tightening as if the walls were closing in.

Me, standing in the doorway, took a hesitant step toward him. "Ash..."

He turned sharply, his eyes blazing. "You knew, didn't you?"

My silence was all the confirmation he needed.

"You knew!" he shouted, his voice echoing in the empty room. "And you didn't tell me? How long, Elleanor? How long have you been keeping this from me?"

He said Elleanor, no Ellie, no Ells...Eleanor...

I flinched but didn't back down. "Ash, listen, I—"

"Don't you dare try to explain this away," he snapped, cutting me off. "You've been acting like we're in this together, like I could trust you, and the whole time, you've been lying to my face!"

My eyes filled with tears, but I kept my voice steady. "I didn't know how to tell you, okay? I was trying to protect you!"

Ash laughed bitterly, running a hand through his hair. "Wow! Protect me? From what? The truth? Omega? You think I can't handle it?" his said sarcastically, repeating my words.

"It's not about what you can handle!" I shot back. "It's about what you deserve. I didn't want you to find out like this. I thought if I could figure out a way to stop them first, you wouldn't have to—"

"Stop them?" Ash interrupted, his voice dripping with sarcasm. "Elleanor, they've already won. Look at me. I'm not even a real person. I'm just... a damn experiment."

“You’re not just an experiment,” I said fiercely, stepping closer to him. “You’re more than whatever they tried to make you. You’re Ash. The guy who fights for what’s right, who cares about people even when it’s hard. None of that is fake.”

Ash shook his head, his jaw clenching. “How do you know that, Ellie? How do you know any of this is real? Maybe I’m just... programmed to be this way.”

“Because I know you,” I said, my voice soft but steady. “I know the way you always try to make people laugh, even when you’re hurting. I know the way you look at me when you think I’m not paying attention. And I know that no amount of programming could fake the way you make me feel.”

My words hung in the air, and for a moment, Ash couldn’t bring himself to respond. He wanted to believe me, but the doubt clawed at him, relentless and suffocating.

"Ash they can control our minds but not our hearts"

"You should've told me," he said finally, his voice quieter now but still heavy with hurt.

I nodded, tears spilling down my cheeks. "I know. And I'm sorry. I was scared, Ash. I didn't want to lose you."

Ash stared at me, his emotions warring inside him. Anger. Betrayal. Sadness. And beneath it all, a flicker of something else—something he wasn't ready to name yet.

"You didn't lose me," he said eventually, his tone softer. "But this... this changes everything."

I wiped my eyes, my expression gritty. "It doesn't have to. We're still in this together. We'll figure it out, Ash. We'll take Omega down, and then you'll get to decide who you want to be. Not them. Not me. You."

Ash looked at me, his walls cracking just enough to let my words sink in. "And what if I don't like who I am?"

I stepped closer, placing a hand on his arm. "Then we'll deal with that too. But for what it's worth, I already like who you are. And I think you will too, once you stop listening to all this noise in your head."

Ash let out a shaky breath, his shoulders sagging as the fight drained out of him. He looked back at the screen, the damning evidence of his existence still glaring at him.

"I don't know if I can do this," he admitted, his voice barely above a whisper.

I squeezed his arm, my grip firm and reassuring. "You don't have to do it alone."

For the first time since he'd found the file, Ash felt a flicker of hope. It was small, fragile, but it was there. And as he looked into my eyes, he realized that maybe, just maybe, I was right.

We stood together in the dimly lit room, the world outside a storm of chaos and uncertainty. But in that moment, we weren't just fighting Omega. We were fighting for ourselves—and for each other.

Chapter 16: Breaking Chains

Meeting Ava was like walking into a twister. Me and Ash had been following a lead on someone who supposedly hacked into Omega's system before—a mystery hacker known as "Luna spark." The rumours led us to an unrestricted bookstore that smelled like rotten food and regret.

The basement of the bookstore? If I could describe in one word "a total mess". Wires tangled in a corner, screens glowing with code, and cans set like a grave. Right in the middle of it was Ava, cross-legged on the floor, typing furiously while blasting music loud enough to bang the walls.

Ash cleared his throat. "Uh, hey?"

Ava removed her headphones, narrowing her eyes. "Who are you, and why are you in my bat cave?"

I snorted. "Bat cave? Really?"

"Yes, really," Ava shot back. "It's my vibe, okay? Now spill. What do you want?"

"We heard you're the best hacker in Havenport," Ash said, cutting straight to the point. "We need help with Omega."

At the mention of Omega, Ava's face shifted—just a flicker, but I caught it. "Omega, huh? Big bad tech ruining lives left and right. And you two want to do... what, exactly? Bring them down with good intentions?"

I crossed my arms. "We've got plans. We just need someone who knows their way around a server."

"Hmm." Ava tilted her head, studying them. Then, with a sly grin, she said, "Alright, I'm in. But only because I'm bored. And because their hackers are a joke, but the system is something."

Ava's involvement turned our scrappy operation into something... almost professional. She was brilliant, no doubt, but also painfully cocky. One night, while we were holed up in Ash's garage-turned-hideout, Ava casually dropped some major info.

"So, Omega's got this thing called the main key," she said, popping a piece of gum and leaning back in her chair.

Ash frowned. "Main key? What's that?"

Ava spun her tablet around to show us what she found. "Think of it like a skeleton key, but for everything Omega. Labs, control chambers, classified files—you name it."

I leaned closer, my heart racing. "Wait... does that mean we could free the people they've taken?"

Ava grinned. "Bingo. But here's the catch—it's locked up in a hidden lab. Hidden in the forest. Super shady. Security is tight. You're welcome."

Ash straightened. "So, we get the key, and we can break them out."

"Exactly," Ava said, folding her arms. "Hoping you don't die trying."

The night of the mission was dark and cold, the forest alive with the sound of rustling leaves and distant owls. Me, Ash, and Ava crept through the underbrush, Ava leading the way with her tablet glowing faintly.

"Alright," Ava whispered. "We're about fifty feet from the clearing. Motion sensors start here, so move like ninjas."

I frowned. "You realize we're not actually ninjas, right?"

"Speak for yourself," Ava shot back, smirking. "Now shush."

Ash leaned closer to me; his voice low. "Don't worry. I've got your back."

I tried to ignore the way my heart skipped at his words. "Focus, Ash."

When they reached the clearing, my first thought was really? The lab looked more like a haunted house, its steel door the only thing giving away its importance.

"This is it?" I asked, unimpressed.

"What were you expecting? A Barbie house?" Ava replied, rolling her eyes. "Let's just get inside."

Ava worked quickly, her fingers dancing over the device she'd brought. After a few tense moments, the door unlocked with a faint beep.

"Ta-da," Ava said, stepping back. "Ladies first."

The interior was sterile and suffocating, the air thick with the buzz of machines. Rows of filing cabinets and outdated computers filled the space, all of it covered in severe fluorescent light.

"Spread out," Ash said. "We're looking for a safe or anything that could hold the key."

We moved quickly but cautiously, searching through drawers and scanning shelves. My hands trembled as I flipped through a stack of files labelled with disturbing titles like "Subject Conditioning" and "Neurological results."

"Guys, this place is... it's evil," I whispered.

"Focus, Ells," Ash said, though his voice cracked slightly. "We'll deal with it later."

Finally, Ash called out, "Over here!"

Me and Ava rushed over to find him crouched by a small safe, its surface scratched and smashed.

"I guess...someone has already tried opening it."

Maybe Clara's brother tried I remember her mentioning how Samuel was close enough to unravel the truth.

"Let me guess, locked?" Ava said, ignoring me.

"Not for long," Ash replied, grabbing the crowbar.

"Do you think, we can open the safe that easily" I stated,

"So do you have any other plan" Ava countered.

"umm...let me see.."

I saw the same jagged circle with a slit, which was all over Havenport, the slit might be the opening, after trying every possible move I just tapped the box the split became more wide and that was it I just slid the safe and revealed the golden key.

Sometimes why to complicate things.

"so this it" Ash said with relief "the next step is to save my sister and Mia"

"And all the other people which are trapped in this" I continued

---

As we left the lab, the weight of what we had found settled over us.

“So, now what?” Ava asked, breaking the silence.

I tightened my grip on the key. “Now, we finish this. We free them. All of them.”

Ash nodded, his expression hardening. “Mia, my sister—they’re waiting for us.”

Ava raised an eyebrow. “You guys are intense, you know that? But I’m in. Let’s wreck their whole operation.”

I smiled faintly, glancing at Ash. “Together?”

“Together,” he agreed.

With the key in hand and a newfound purpose driving us, we disappeared into the night, ready to take the fight of Omega.

Chapter 17: Fragments of home

The moment was unreal. I couldn't believe Mia was standing right Infront of me, existing and breathing. For months, the thought of my best friend had been a constant ache—a reminder of what Omega had stolen. Now, with Mia holding my arm for balance, that ache shifted to something different, heavier. Maybe relief tangled with guilt.

"Mia, it's me," I whispered, my voice trembling as I placed a hand on Mia's shoulder.

Mia blinked, her eyes unfocused and glassy, as if trying to piece together fragments of a shattered memory. "Ellie?" Her voice cracked, weak, but so unmistakably hers that my heart clenched. "What's going on? Where am I?"

Before I could answer, Ash's sharp voice cut through. "Ells, we don't have time for reunions. They're coming."

I looked over, where Ash stood, his hands gripping the edge of another glass pod. Inside, a young woman with soft features and the same greenish eyes as Ash lay. His sister. I had never seen him like this—his usually steady hands shook, his expression torn between urgency and emotion which were raw.

“Ava!” Ash barked into his earpiece. “How do I get this open?”

Ava’s voice came through, rushed but focused. “Same as before. Use the key on the side panel. Hurry up! That alarm is drawing everyone.”

I turned to Mia, gripping her arms. “Mia, listen to me. You’re safe now, but we need to move. Can you walk?”

Mia swayed slightly but nodded. “I think so.”

“Stay close to me,” I said before running to Ash’s side. He was already unlocking the pod, his breath shallow and uneven.

The chamber hissed, and the glass slid open. Ash’s sister crumpled forward, and he caught her instantly, his arms wrapping around her with a gentleness I hadn’t thought possible.

“Emilia,” Ash whispered, his voice cracking. “Lia, it’s me. It’s Ash. Wake up.”

The sound of her name seemed to mingled something in me. Emilia’s eyes fluttered open, her gaze blurred and confused. “Ash?” she murmured, her voice faint.

“Yeah, it’s me,” Ash said, his words rushed but warm. “You’re safe now. I’ve got you.”

I felt a lump form in my throat, watching Ash’s walls crumble as he held his sister. The usual mischievous Ash, who always drag the weight of their mission with patient determination, was now just a brother—desperate, vulnerable, and completely human.

But the moment was short-lived. The sound of heavy boots pounding down the corridor snapped me back to reality.

"They're here," I said,

Ash looked up, his jaw tightening. "We can't fight them off and get out with Mia and Lia like this. Ava, options?"

Ava's response was quick. "There's a service exit two stories down. I'm overriding the locks, but you've got to move fast."

"Got it," Ash said, lifting Emilia into his arms like she weighed nothing. He turned to me. "You lead. I'll cover the back."

I nodded, gripping Mia's arm to steady her as we began to run.

The halls blurred as we navigated the unsolved maze of Omega's facility. The alarms were loud now, flashing red lights casting spooky shadows on the walls. My heart pounded; my senses sharp with every step.

Mia stumbled, and I caught her just in time. “I’ve got you,” I said, my voice firm despite the chaos around them.

Behind me, Ash’s footsteps were steady, even with the added weight of his sister in his arms. “Ellie,” he called out, his tone urgent. “Keep moving. Don’t stop.”

The sound of gunfire echoed down the hallway, making my blood run cold.

“They’re aiming on you!” Ava shouted. “Take the next left!”

I turned left, practically dragging Mia along. my lungs burned as if it was on fire, and every instinct screamed at me to turn back and help Ash. But i knew better. If I stopped, they’d lose everything.

When they burst through the service exit, the cold dawn air hit me like a slap. I gasped, dragging Mia forward until they were clear of the doorway.

Ash emerged seconds later, his face set in satisfaction. Behind him, the distant shouts of guards grew louder.

“Ava, we’re out!” Ash said, lowering Emilia gently onto the ground.

“I’m locking down the exit, but it won’t hold for long,” Ava replied. “Your exist point is half a mile north. I’ve got a car waiting.”

“Half a mile,” I muttered, glancing at Mia and Emilia. Neither of them was in any condition to run.

Ash knelt beside his sister, brushing a strand of hair from her face. “Lia, can you hear me?”

She nodded weakly, her voice barely a whisper. “You found me.”

“Of course, I did,” Ash said, his voice breaking. “I’m never leaving you again.”

My chest tightened at the sight of them. I turned to Mia, who was leaning heavily against a tree. “Mia, are you okay?”

"I think so," Mia said, though her voice was shaky. Her eyes darted around, taking in their surroundings. "Ellie... what's happening? Who are these people?"

I hesitated, unsure how to explain the nightmare Mia had been trapped in. "I'll tell you everything. But first, we need to get out of here."

The trek to the exist point was slow and unbearable. Me and Ash took turns supporting Mia and Emilia, every sound in the forest felt like a threat, every shadow a possible enemy.

When they finally reached the waiting car, I nearly collapsed with relief. Ava was leaning against the hood, her usual smirk replaced by a look of genuine concern. "Damn," Ava said, her gaze sweeping over the group. "You all look like you've been through hell."

"Because we have," Ash muttered, helping Emilia into the back seat.

As we loaded into the car, I sat beside Mia, who was staring out the window with a expression I couldn't read. "Hey," I said softly, "You're safe now. I promise."

Mia turned to me, tears streaming down her face. "I don't remember everything, Ellie. But I know it was bad. I don't know if I'll ever be okay."

My heart shattered like glass, but I squeezed Mia's hand tightly. "You don't have to be okay right now. Just... stay with me. That's all I need."

In the back seat, Ash glanced back at his sister, who had fallen asleep against his shoulder. His expression was unreadable, but I could see the weight of everything they'd been through carved into his features.

As the car sped away from the facility, leaving the horrors of Omega behind, I felt a strange mix of hope and dread. They had won a small victory, but the fight was far from over.

Chapter 18: The Breaking Point

The air in the room which felt kind of secretive was heavy with an odd silence, a suffocating kind of quiet that likely to leak into my bones. The deeper we dig, the more I felt like we were walking through the echoes of a nightmare—one where the walls themselves experienced or witness to unsaid horrors.

"Ells, you good?" Ash's voice was soft but edged with concern. He walked close behind me, his flashlight cutting through the dim corridor.

"I'm fine," I lied, but the trembling in my hands said otherwise.

Behind us, Ava muttered, "This place looks like it's straight out of a dystopian fever dream. If we run into a zombie, I'm backing out." She tried to sound cool, but even her sarcasm lacked its usual bite.

Mia was quiet, her arms wrapped around herself as she shuffled along. I glanced back at Mia, guilt troubling within. She shouldn't even be here, not after everything she'd been through. None of them should.

"This is it," Ava said shortly, stopping in front of a steel door. The faint tinkle of machinery buzzed behind it. She tapped on her tablet, her fingers flying across the screen. "Give me a sec. This lock's a little trickier than the others."

I leaned against the wall, trying to steady my breathing. I caught Ash's eye, and for a moment, the noise in my head calmed. He didn't say anything, just gave me one of those looks—the kind that made me feel seen, grounded.

Ava let out a low whistle. "And... we're in." The door hissed open, revealing a vast chamber filled with rows upon rows of glass pods.

I stepped inside, my stomach lurching. Each shell held a person, their faces creepily still, as if they were just sleeping. But the wires attached to their temples and the faint glow of screens above them told a different story.

“What the hell is this?” Ash said, his voice tight.

“It’s... worse than I thought,” Ava muttered, her earlier boldness gone. She pointed to the screens, where streams of data scrolled endlessly. “They’re... collecting memories. Selling them. These people... they’re living archives.”

My knees threatened to clasp. “So, they’re... alive?”

“Technically, yeah,” Ava replied. “But their minds? Their identities? All being stripped away and turned into data points.”

I felt sick. I turned to Ash, who was staring at the shells with a clenched jaw. “Ash...”

“Don’t,” he said, his voice low. “Don’t say it.”

But I had to. “What if we’re next? What if... what if they’ve already done this to us?

The journal had hinted at it—a passage about subjects being monitored even outside of the labs, their interactions and relationships manipulated for further study. I had dismissed it as paranoia at first. But now, standing in this room of stolen lives, I wasn’t so sure.

Ava’s tablet beeped, and she frowned at the screen. “Uh, guys? I’m picking up files... on us. Like, detailed files.”

“What do you mean, ‘files?” Ash demanded, moving to stand beside her.

“Exactly what it sounds like,” Ava said, her tone grim. She tapped a few buttons, and a series of documents appeared on the tablet. “Look—Ellie, Ash, Mia, even me. They’ve been tracking us. Our decisions, our emotions... everything.”

My heart stopped when I saw her name on the screen. The file contained a timeline of my life—photos, journal entries, even memories I didn't recognize as my own.

"This can't be real," I whispered, my voice barely audible.

"It's real," Ava said, her voice softer now. "And it gets worse." She hesitated, then swiped to another file. "Ellie... look at this."

The screen displayed a series of interactions between me and Ash, each one studied and tagged with labels like "emotional attachment," "trust level," and "romantic inclination."

"They've been watching us," I said, my voice shaking. "Every moment, every word... It was all... part of their experiment."

Ash grabbed the tablet, his face darkening as he read the file. "So what? They think they can measure how we feel about each other with data points?" He threw the tablet onto the table, the screen cracking on impact. “That doesn’t change anything.”

My eyes stared at him, tears streaming down “Doesn’t it? Ash, what if this—us—isn’t real? What if they planned it? Manipulated it?”

He stepped closer, his hands on my shoulders. “Ellie, listen to me. I don’t care what they did or didn’t do. What I feel when I’m with you—that’s real. I know it is.”

I shook my head, pulling away. “How can you be so sure? How can we trust anything anymore?”

“Because it’s not about them,” he said, his voice steady but filled with emotion. “It’s about us. What we’ve been through together. What we’ve fought for. That’s real, Ells. It has to be.”

Mia, who had been silent until now, stepped forward. “Ellie, you’ve always been the one to believe in people. Don’t let them take that away from you. Don't let them win."

I glanced at Mia then Ash, and others who had risked everything to be here. They were more than data points. More than subjects in someone else's experiment.

I took a shaky breath, wiping my eyes. "Okay," I said softly. "Okay."

Ash exhaled, relief washing over his face. "We're not letting them take anything else from us."

Ava cleared her throat. "Hate to interrupt this heartfelt moment, but we've got company. Lots of it."

The sound of footsteps echoed down the corridor, growing louder by the second.

Ash picked up a nearby pipe, his expression hardening. "Then let's finish this."

I nodded; my fear replaced by determination. We weren't just fighting for ourselves anymore. We were fighting for everyone who had been trapped, manipulated, and erased by Omega.

As the doors burst open and the guards poured in, I gripped Ash's hand tightly. Whatever happened next, we would face it together.

And this time, we would win.

Chapter 19: The Sacrifice

The room was a chaotic blend of glowing screens and buzzing machinery, the core of Omega's operations. I stood like a statue, my eyes fixed on the figure standing Infront of me. The leader of Omega—a shadowy, mysterious presence—spoke with a calmness that only made the weight of the moment more unbearable.

"You've made it farther than I expected," the leader said, their voice low and even. "But now comes the real test."

my fist clenched. "Test? You've ruined lives—turned people into nothing more than data—and you think this is some kind of game?"

The leader stepped closer; my face partially illuminated by the pale glow of the central AI system. “It’s never been a game. It’s progress. And now, you have a choice. Destroy this system, and every memory it’s ever touched will be lost. That includes you, your friends, the people you’ve saved. Or...” They gestured to the buzzing AI. “You can walk away. Leave it intact. Keep your memories. Keep your reality.”

My breath hitched. The weight of the decision pressed down on my chest, threatening to crush me.

“Ells...” Ash’s voice pulled me back. He was standing behind me, his hand on the edge of the control panel. His usually steady gaze was wavering, a storm of emotions flickering in his eyes. “You don’t have to decide this alone.”

I turned to him, tears blurring my vision. “How can I choose, Ash? If I destroy it, I’ll be erasing everything. What if I lose you? What if I lose us?”

Ash took a step closer, his voice softer now. “And what if…what we have is strong enough to survive this? You said it yourself—we’re more than what they’ve done to us. We’re more than data.”

The leader smirked, his voice cutting through the tension like a knife. “Beautiful words. But are you willing to bet everything on them? On him?”

My head snapped back toward his. “Shut up.” my voice trembled with anger and fear.

Ava’s voice crackled through the comms. “Uh, not to interrupt your existential crisis, but we’ve got a timeline here. Whatever you’re gonna do, do it fast. This place is not earthquake-proof.”

Mia, standing near the doorway, called out, “Ellie, we trust you. Whatever you choose, we’re with you.”

My hands hovered over the controls, her thoughts twisting. Memories of Ash’s laugh,

Mia's loyalty, Ava's humour—all of it could disappear in an instant.

I turned to Ash, tears spilling down my cheeks. "What if I make the wrong choice?"

Ash reached out, his hands gently embracing my face. "Then we deal with it. Together. But this—" He glanced at the glowing core of the AI. "This isn't living, Ells. Not for them. Not for us. If you don't stop it, they win."

I searched his face, my heart breaking. He looked so sure, so steady, even as I felt myself falling apart.

I nodded, my voice barely a whisper. "Okay."

The decision was made. My trembling fingers moved over the control panel as the leader's calm facade cracked.

"You don't know what you're doing!" they shouted, stepping toward me.

Ash moved between them, his stance firm. “Back off.”

The leader hesitated, their eyes narrowing. “You’ll regret this. All of you.”

“Maybe,” I said, my voice stronger now. “But at least it’ll be my choice. Not yours.”

With one final press of a button, the core began to glow brighter, alarms blaring as the system initiated its self-destruct sequence.

“Ellie, we’ve got to move!” Ava shouted through the comms.

The ground beneath them rumbled, the walls trembling as the facility started to collapse. I turned to run, but Ash grabbed my arm, pulling me back just as a chunk of remains fell where I stood.

“You okay?” he asked, his voice frantic.

“I’m fine!” I shouted over the chaos.

The two of us hurried toward the exit, dodging falling remains and sparks flying from bare wires. My heart pounded, my mind racing with the weight of what I had just done.

As we reached the final exit, the ceiling above them groaned.

"Go!" Ash shouted, shoving me forward.

I stumbled, turning just in time to see a beam collapse behind me, trapping Ash on the other side.

"Ash!" I screamed, my voice breaking.

"I'm fine!" he called back, though he was clutching his shoulder, blood leaking through his fingers. "Get out of here!"

"I'm not leaving you!"

He gave me a look, one filled with so much love and pain it nearly broke me. "Ellie, you have to. Please."

Tears streamed down my face as I nodded, my heart shattering. "I'll come back for you. I promise."

I made it out just as the facility collapsed in on itself, a deafening roar echoing through the forest. I fell to my knees, gasping for air, my hands trembling as I stared at the remains.

Minutes felt like hours before I saw movement. Ash stumbled out, bloodied but alive, his eyes searching for me.

“Ellie,” he said, his voice hoarse.

I ran to him, throwing my arms around him as sobs wracked my body. “I thought I lost you.”

“I’m here,” he whispered, holding me tightly. “I’m here.”

But as he pulled back, I saw the confusion in his eyes. “Ellie… I… I don’t remember…”

my heart sank. “What?”

He shook his head, his voice breaking. “You. Us. I know you’re important to me, but… it’s like there’s a hole where the memories should be.”

I bit my lip, fighting back tears. “It’s okay,” I said, my voice trembling. “We’ll figure it out. Together.”

He nodded, though his eyes were filled with uncertainty.

As the sun rose over the remains, I realized the cost of our victory. We had stopped Omega, but the price had been pieces of ourselves—pieces we might never get back.

But as I looked at Ash, his hand still holding me despite the emptiness in his eyes, I knew one thing for sure.

We still had each other. And that was enough to start again.

Chapter 20: The Betrayal Beneath the Surface

I sat on the damp, crumbling pier, staring out at the endless ocean, the salty air clinging to my skin. For the first time in weeks, everything was same. Too still. My mind raced with flashbacks of the past months: the journal, the experiments, the secrets—everything leading to this moment. And Ash. Always Ash.

“I can’t believe it’s finally over,” I muttered to myself, my voice barely audible against the crashing waves.

“Is it?”

The voice that spoke made my blood run cold. It was a voice…, one that had whispered promises and shared fears. I turned slowly to see Ash standing behind me, his hands stuffed in his jacket pockets, his face unreadable.

"Ash? What do you mean?" I asked, my voice trembling.

He stepped closer, the light from the sun casting sharp shadows across his face. "Ells, I need you to understand something. None of this—us, the mission, the 'victory'—none of it was what you thought."

My heart skipped a beat, my chest tightening. "What are you saying?"

Ash took a deep breath, as if the weight of his own words threatened to crush him. "I'm not just some victim of Omega. I'm not some guy trying to bring them down. Ellie, I am Omega."

The words hit me like a bullet train. I stumbled back, my eyes widen with disbelief. "What? No. That's not—no."

"It's true," he said, his voice calm, almost disconnected. "The experiments, the tech, the memory manipulation—it was all me.

And you? You were always part of the plan."

My knees were numb, and I collapsed onto the pier. "You're lying. You have to be lying. This can't be real."

Ash crouched in front of me, his expression soft but stiff. "Ellie, I never wanted to hurt you. But you were the perfect subject. The one who could prove everything I've worked for."

My hands clenched into fists as I tried to make sense of his words. "Why? Why me? What did I ever do to deserve this? And why would you destroy your own company?"

"You were different, Ells," Ash said, his voice laced with an almost cruel affection. "Your mind, your emotions—they were unlike anyone else's. You had this way of questioning everything, of seeing through the lies. I knew if I could break you, if I could manipulate you, then the system was flawless. You became the ultimate test subject."

my eyes burned with tears, but I refused to let them fall. “You used me. Everything we went through—was it all fake?”

everything, every word? Every emotions? Every laughter?

Ash hesitated, a flicker of something—regret?—crossing his face. “Not all of it. I didn’t expect to... care about you. That wasn’t part of the plan.”

I laughed bitterly, the sound hollow and sharp. “Oh, great. So I was just a science experiment with a sprinkle of feelings thrown in. How touching.”

Ash stood, pacing along the edge of the pier. “Ellie, you don’t understand. omega wasn’t supposed to be evil. It was meant to fix things. To create a world where emotions couldn’t destroy people, where pain could be erased. But humans are messy. We hold on to hurt, to love, to things that make us weak. I wanted to change that.”

“And what? Turn us all into robots? Perfect little puppets?” I snapped, my voice rising.

“I wanted to make you stronger!” he shouted, his composure cracking for the first time. “Don’t you get it? If I could control emotions, I could control pain. I could stop people from destroying themselves.”

I shook my head, my voice trembling with anger. “You don’t get to decide that for anyone, Ash. You don’t get to play god.”

The weight of his betrayal pressed down on me like a tidal wave. Every moment we had shared—every laugh, every touch, every stolen glance—it all felt like it was nothing now.

“But why pretend to be one of us? Why go through all of this with me?” I asked, my voice barely above a whisper.

“Because I needed you to trust me,” he admitted. “I needed you to see me as the victim, the ally. If you’d known who I really was, you'd never have let me get close. And I needed to be close, Ellie. To see how far I could push you, how much I could change you."

My chest ached, the tears finally spilling over. "So that's it? That's all I was to you? A project?"

Ash looked away, his jaw tightening. "No. You were more than that. You still are. That's why I'm telling you the truth now. Because you deserve to know."

I stood up; my legs shaky but I manged somehow. "You think this is some kind of a truce? That telling me the truth makes up for everything you've done?"

"I'm not looking for truce," he said quietly. "I'm looking for understanding."

"Well, you won't get it from me," I spat, my voice sharp with anger and pain. "You might have created this mess, Ash, but you don't get to control me anymore. I'm done."

As I turned to leave, Ash reached out, his hand brushing my arm. “Ellie, wait. If you walk away now, you’ll never know the full truth.”

I froze, my heart pounding. “The truth? You mean the truth you’ve been twisting and hiding this whole time?”

Ash’s voice softened, almost pleading. “There’s more to this than you know. More than even, I can explain right now. But if you leave, you’ll never understand why I did all of this.”

I pulled away; my voice steady despite the tears streaming down my face. “I don’t need to understand you, Ash. I just need to survive you.”

As I walked away, my mind raced with a storm of emotions—anger, betrayal, sadness, and a sliver of something I hated to admit: love. Despite everything, I couldn’t deny the connection we had shared, even if it had been built on lies.

"Ellie, you need know the whole truth" Ash said, "you can't just walk away..."

My mind was exhausted so I just sat down on the bench.

Ash sat beside me; his hands clasped together as he began to unravel the story.

"I wasn't born into Omega," he started. "I wasn't some genius employed for my brilliance. I was just a kid trying to survive in a world that didn't care about people like me. Omega found me, offered me a purpose, a way to matter. At first, I believed in what they were doing—pushing the boundaries of human understanding, unlocking potential no one else could see."

He paused; his gaze distant. "But then I started to see the cracks. The way they treated people like numbers, like data points to be manipulated. I tried to convince myself it was for the greater good, that the sacrifices were worth it. Until I met you."

I frowned; my arms crossed protectively over my chest. "And what was so special about me?"

"You reminded me of everything I'd forgotten," Ash said, his voice thick with emotion. "You were brave, curious, stubborn as hell. You saw the world differently, and you made me see it differently too. At first, I thought I could just keep playing my role, keep following orders. But the more time I spent with you, the harder it became to lie and the urge to destroy Omega code."

"Then why did you?" I demanded, my voice cracking. "Why didn't you just tell me the truth?"

"Because I was afraid," Ash admitted. "Afraid of losing you. Afraid of what Omega would do to you if I stepped out of line. They were watching us, Ellie. Every move we made, every word we said—it was all being monitored. I thought... I thought I could protect you if I stayed in control."

I shook my head, my emotions fighting within me. "And yet, here we are. Me, finding out everything I believed was a lie. You, standing there asking for forgiveness. What am I supposed to do with that, Ash?"

He looked at me, his eyes filled with something I couldn't quite name—hope, desperation, regret. "Do whatever feels right. Hate me, yell at me, walk away. But please, Ellie... Don't let this be the end. Don't let Omega win by tearing us apart."

I stared at him for what felt like an eternity, my mind and heart in chaos. I wanted to scream, to cry, to run. But beneath all the hurt and anger, there was something else. A tiny, stubborn ember that refused to go out.

"Do you really regret it?" I asked quietly.

"More than anything," Ash said without hesitation.

I took a deep breath, my chest tight. "I don't know if I can forgive you, Ash. Not now, maybe not ever. But… I think I understand why you did what you did. And maybe that's a start."

Ash nodded, his eyes glistening. "That's all I can ask for."

As we sat in the silence that followed, the weight of their shared past lingered, but so did the fragile possibility of something new. Something real.

And for the first time, I felt like I was finally seeing the truth—not just about Ash, but about myself.

Acknowledgement

Writing this novel has been an unforgettable journey, one I could not have completed without the unwavering support of the incredible people in my life,

A special thank you to my dear readers, you are the heart of this story. Your love for the twists, turns, plots and mysteries is what brought *Hidden Echoes* to life.

Finally to everyone who ever felt like an outsider in their own world: this one's for you may you always find the strength in the unknown, courage in the uncertain and hope in the hidden echoes of your heart

With love and gratitude,

Sakina patanwala.